Also by Carole Walker Carter

<u>Aztarian Series</u>
AZTARA, The Mastel Kingdom
SURTEES, Science Rules
AZTARA, A Galactic Love Story
AZTARA, Secrets Revealed

<u>Evers and McFarlan Detective Series</u>
Final Alumni
Shadowy Faces
Nine Points of a Circle

<u>Fantasy Books</u>
The Child Rowanda, Little Dragon
The Child Rowanda, Return to Arolsen
The Child Rowanda, Underworld
Khaos, Lord of the Thunder Dragons
The Child Rowanda, Dragon Princess

<u>Children's Books on www.walkercarter.com</u>
Tinker Robot
Grandma's Magic Scarf
Granny Nell
Alec the Astronaut

Childhood Stories My Dad Told Me

Carole Walker Carter

WALKER CARTER PUBLISHING, LLC

Copyright © 2018 by Carole Walker Carter
All Rights Reserved

No part of this publication may be reproduced, or stored in a retrieval system, or transmitted in any form or by any means, electronically, mechanically, photocopying, recording, or otherwise, without written permission of the publisher. For information regarding permission, send an email to adminhost@walkercarter.com, Attention Permission Department.

Cover Design by Donald & Carole Carter

Childhood Stories My Dad Told Me / by Carole Walker Carter

ISBN 978-1-947734-81-4

9 8 7 6 5 4 3 2 1 17 18 19 20 21

[Young Adult, Family, Nebraska, Depression Era, Farm Life, Country]

WALKER CARTER PUBLISHING, LLC

Please check out my website at www.walkercarter.com

To my girls Jennifer and Lisa, my grandson Nixon, my granddaughter Alex and my husband, Don.

In memory of my mother and dad, Elda and Dean Walker.

I will always love you!!!

ACKNOWLEDGMENTS

I wrote this book in cooperation with my best friend and husband, Donald E. Carter, author of _Concurrent Engineering, Product Development Environment_ business books. Don's experience helped to research all the technical information in this book.

Janis Lane supported me with my writing by cheering me on to tell my stories. Don and I worked diligently to edit this book over the past year.

My girls, Jennifer and Lisa Coyle, provided several useful resource books. Without their support and prodding, this book may still be in draft form.

Janel Walker and Linda Sturgill, my sisters, frequently ask for more information about the stories our Dad told me.

Special thanks to all those that donated to my GoFundMe page, Linda Sturgill, Elda Walker, Janel Walker, Judy Mathiesen, Linda Maddex, Afsaneh Fowler, and Carol Royce Davidson. These donations kick-started my venture by allowing me to acquire editing and review tools, ISBN numbers, audio equipment, and final publication costs.

TABLE OF CONTENTS

CHAPTER ONE

"Boys," hollered Mama as she stepped onto the rickety old front porch allowing the screen door to slam behind her. "Boys, come on and eat breakfast. You can finish your chores after you eat."

Going back inside the small farmhouse, Mama went to the wood-burning stove. She reached into the oven and took out the cast iron pan filled with biscuits. Mama started her chores earlier that morning. It was going to be a hot day, so cooking and baking would need to be done early in the morning. For Mama, that meant making five loaves of bread and maybe some sweet rolls if there was enough flour. She would ask Papa to pick up another bag of flour when he went into town right after breakfast.

Papa came into the farmhouse with the two boys tagging along behind him. "Did you wash up at the pump before you came in? If not, get out there and wash up. Make sure you wash all the way to your elbows," Papa instructed.

Taking a seat at the family table, which Papa made himself from a tree he cut down when the family first moved onto the acreage. The house already existed, as well as the barn, the chicken coop, a pig barn, and another outbuilding used to store implements and other equipment. No furniture was left when the previous family moved. The word around town was that the family was moving west.

Town folk said they just couldn't stay on the farm once they lost two of their children to drowning down at the river.

The two boys entered loudly, pushing and shoving each other in rough play. "That is enough," said Papa in a stern voice. The boys immediately settled down and came and sat at the table.

Abby was busy helping her mother put food on the table. At the tender age of four, she was still considered a working member of the family and no longer treated like a baby. Her job was to help Mama with all the chores. Mama would continue to teach her how to make bread, wash clothes, wring them out and hang them on the line for the sun to dry. The next day would start the tedious job of ironing the clothes. Abby hated ironing day, even though Mama only gave her a few easy items to iron.

"Daniel, please pour cups of milk for you, your brother and Abby," Mama asked politely.

"Aww, Mama, that is woman's work," Daniel said, making no effort to get to his feet.

A smack alongside the head from Papa, caused Daniel to jump to his feet without hesitation. The hit didn't hurt. It was a warning to do as he was told.

"I don't want to ever hear any backtalk to your mama again. Do you understand? You aren't too old for me to take behind the woodshed, you know." Papa got up and came to the stove to carry the biscuits Mama had just taken out. Abby quickly brought in a mound of butter Mama churned the previous day and stored in the spring house.

Eggs were sizzling on the top of the stove, and Mama expertly lifted each egg without breaking the yolk and placed them on individual plates. Bacon was already piled high on a separate platter in the center of the table. William was chewing a long piece of bacon that he snuck off the plate while Papa was reprimanding Daniel. William only chewed when he knew his father's eyes were elsewhere. He knew a smack on the head would be his punishment as well if Papa realized he had stolen an extra piece of bacon.

Mama and Abby sat down, and everyone bowed their heads. Saying grace was expected at all meals. Mama was pious, and Papa was a good man. They would set the right example for their children.

Trying not to talk with his mouth full, Daniel told Papa that the cows were milked and turned out to graze in the pasture. "We will slop the hogs right after breakfast," Daniel said as he pushed another bite of biscuit into his mouth.

Papa glared at Daniel. 'Mind your manners, boy. You weren't taught to talk with your mouth full. After you slop the hogs, hurry and get Maud and Molly hitched to the wagon. I will drop you and your brother off at school when I drive into town."

"Yes, Sir. But Papa, I noticed Maud is favoring her left front hoof. I don't know if she has a stone bruise or what. Would you rather I hitch up Saul with Molly? I know he is old, but I think he can make it to town and back if you are not hauling a heavy load." Daniel pushed his plate away and looked to see if his brother was ready to finish the chores.

William imitated his brother and pushed his plate back as well. Waiting for permission to leave the table, all four eyes were on Papa.

"Daniel, when you get home from school, I want you to check out Maud better. Do a full evaluation. I need to know when she will be able to plow or if I am going to need to borrow a mule from Zack, down the road." Papa nodded for the boys to leave, and he resumed eating his breakfast as the boys went.

Mama smiled. "Daniel is getting to know his way around horses, isn't he? You have taught your boys well. They are an asset here on the farm."

Papa smiled back at his beautiful wife. He remembered the young bride he married and how even after having three children and being pregnant with the fourth, looked as pretty as the day he married her. He was never sure what she had seen in him, but he counted his lucky stars each and every day of the twelve years of their marriage.

"Is there anything else you need from town? I know you want some flour. Do you need sugar or baking soda? I will be at the general store most of the time I am in town. I plan to be home by lunch, so I won't be gone long. Just give me a list, and I will have Martin gather what you need. Do you have the eggs packed carefully for travel? I would hate to have them break on that bumpy dirt road."

"Yes, Dear," Mama said as she gathered up the dishes to be washed. The kettle was already heating on the wood-burning stove for the dishwashing water. Abby knew her job would be to dry the dishes and put the ones away in the cupboards that she could reach. "The boxes are on the porch with Shep guarding them from any egg-sucking varmints. That dog is worth a million to me."

Papa got up from the table, thanked his wife and daughter for an excellent breakfast, and went to see if the boys needed help hitching up the wagon. Papa knew Saul could be grouchy. Saul resented being asked to come out of retirement. At the age of thirty, Saul was considered an old horse.

Saul was Papa's horse since he was a teen. Papa felt his horse deserved to be put out to pasture. The two of them went through many adventures together, but now Saul was old and tired. Papa hated to ask the old guy to help pull the wagon even one more time, but until Maud was better, Saul would need to earn his oats.

Saul was a big buckskin horse in his younger years. He stood 17 hands tall. His coat would shine in the sun like buttercream, but now his coat was dull and hung on the tired old frame. Bones seemed to poke out everywhere, making him appear like a scarecrow's horse. In Papa's eyes, Saul would always be big and handsome. He smiled when he saw Saul was raising his head up so high that the boys were unable to slip the harness over his head. Walking up with a handful of oats, Saul sniffed the air and immediately lowered his head for the snack. Papa took the harness and slipped it over his head while the horse contentedly munched on his favorite food.

Molly stood hitched and ready to go. Maud watched with interest from her stall. Nickering to her barn mate, Papa knew the two horses would protest the separation. Being raised together since foals, the two were perfectly matched in more ways than their dark brown coloring. They moved like a team even when out in the pasture.

Lifting William up onto the seat, he told Daniel to drive the wagon over to the house and load the boxes of eggs onto the back. "Be careful with those eggs. I don't want a single one cracked. Also, make sure you push them close to the seats, so none of the boxes will vibrate off the wagon when we are traveling. I want to trade those eggs for a few provisions for your mother. If all the eggs get to the general store without a crack, I may just get you and William a peppermint stick," Papa said to encourage the boys to be careful. Candy was not given out often, so it was a special treat.

Papa had a few more chores to attend to himself, so he knew the boys would be changed into their school clothes and would be ready to leave as soon as he walked the distance back to the house. Papa was not kept waiting. William and Daniel seated in the back of the wagon, ready to leave when Papa made the walk across the open expanse from the barn to the house.

Chickens were free-roaming around the yard. Shep knew better than to chase the chickens. He lay under the tree, watching their movements. His job was to protect the chickens from foxes, rats, or raccoons. Even other farm dogs were sent home with their tails between their legs if they made the mistake of entering Shep's domain. A gentle shepherd by nature, Shep was a great babysitter and playmate for the children, but he would become fearsome if a perceived enemy should appear. Shep bore the scars of more than one bite from animals that tangled with him, but Shep always came out on the top.

As Papa clicked with his tongue to the team to move out, Shep got to his feet. He loved to run behind the team and wagon up the dirt hill to the end of the property line. Barking and giving chase, Shep escorted the wagon to the top of the hill. Wagging his tail, he gave one final bark and turned around to attend to his job at the farm.

Abby was in the yard when he returned. One of her least favorite chores was attending to the chickens. It was too early to gather eggs, to Abby's relief. The hens were not good about giving up the eggs they laid, and Abby hated to be pecked when she would reach under the hens to take the eggs away. Well, that would be later in the day. Right now, she needed to scatter corn for the hens and the rooster.

Shep, seeing the little girl, barked a greeting and rushed to accompany her to the waiting flock of chickens. Abby threw small handfuls in all directions and watched the hens scramble to be the first one there to peck at the kernels of corn. The hens would peck any other hen that got too close to the morsel they had their eyes on. It was the same each and every morning with the lesser hens being chased away time and time again. Abby felt sorry for the hens at the bottom of the pecking order and tried hopelessly to get them a pile of their own, but they would always be chased away. She knew they got enough to survive, but it seemed so sad they got so little.

Abby knew her mother would be waiting for her to help with the baking, but she also knew her mother would not mind if she played with Shep for a few minutes. Finding a stick, she threw it as far as her little arms would allow. Shep's eyes would follow the stick in the air and usually caught it before it hit the ground. Happily, he would bring the stick back for Abby to throw as many times as she had time to do.

"Abby, wash your hands before you come in to help with the baking. That stick is dirty, and I don't want anyone getting sick because you forgot to wash your hands," Mama said from the opened door.

Abby knew that was her reminder to stop playing with Shep and to come in immediately. Baking took all day, but Mama always let her have time to play under the tree with the kittens. The warning each day was not to have the kittens close to her face and to wash thoroughly after playing with them. Mama scared Abby with warnings about ringworm. Abby didn't know what it was, but by the way, Mama said the word, it must be horrible.

The smell of baked bread filled the little farmhouse with a heavenly aroma. There were two rooms upstairs and one-bedroom downstairs. The small living room had a wood-burning stove to help heat the house. The wood-burning stove in the kitchen aided as well, even though it was used primarily for cooking and baking.

The boys came loudly into the house after school was out. Mama had put buttered bread on a plate waiting for them when they arrived home. After wolfing down the bread, Mama told them to change out of their school clothes and get right to their chores. With limited school clothing, the boys knew they would need to wear the same shirt and trousers for several days.

Abby tagged along to the barn behind her older brothers. Daniel was big for his age. William, even though only ten months younger than Daniel, seemed several years younger due to his small size. Abby loved her brothers and wanted to be with them all the time, even though they teased her mercilessly.

Pulling up milking stools, Daniel aimed the teat directly at Abby, squirting her with warm milk right out of the cow's udder. "Stop that! You are getting milk in my hair, and I will have to wash it, or it will stink like sour milk."

"Why don't you just learn to open your mouth wide like I do?" joked William, as Daniel directed the spray of milk into his brother's mouth.

Abby giggled as William opened his mouth wider and wider to accommodate the stream of warm milk. The cats meowed around the boy's feet, hoping for their milk treat, as well.

"Papa said all milk is going to be pasteurized soon. He said some doctors said you could get sick from raw milk. If that is true, why don't the calves all get sick?" Abby asked in all earnest.

Daniel answered his little sister. "Sometimes the calves do get sick. You have seen Papa treat the calves for scours."

"Daniel, you weren't listening when the teacher told us scours is from many factors, such as the cow's poor nutrition the last month before having the calf, or from the calf being in crowded and dirty stalls or yards. It isn't from the mother's milk," William, the scholar of the family recited.

'Could be from lots of things, but that doesn't mean those bacterial bugs in milk isn't one of them," Daniel countered.

"Are you going to get scours, William? You just drank lots of cow's milk, and it wasn't pasteurized," Abby whimpered.

"No way! I am too tough. It will take more than some cow's milk to kill me, so don't worry about me," William said.

The boys moved from cow to cow, stopping only when the buckets were full. As the boys emptied the milk into larger containers, Abby played in the straw with the kittens.

"Did you watch that goofy boy, Dillon, playing baseball all by himself. I think it is the strangest thing how he pretends to hit the ball and then run all the bases when he doesn't even have a bat or a ball. That kid is not all there. I feel bad for his sister. She is always

20

embarrassed for him," Daniel said aside to William, hoping their sister was not hearing them.

"It is creepy. Dillon can't read, write, or do his numbers. He is even older than you, Daniel. I heard he got kicked in the head by a mule, and now he has no sense."

Daniel said, "He ain't normal, that is for sure. Do you think we should try to play a real game of baseball with him? Who knows, he might actually be good at it. It would make his sister happy if someone played with him so she could do something else except babysitting him all day."

"*Daniel has a girlfriend. Daniel has a girlfriend,*" William sang in a sing-song way. "Does Becky know you are sweet on her?"

"Oh, shut up, William. You don't know a thing. Just cuz I feel bad for Becky doesn't mean I want to marry her."

With William dancing around singing his little ditty and making smooching noises, Daniel could finally take no more. Knocking his milking stool backward, Daniel sprung to his feet, chasing his little brother around the barn while Abby screamed in fright.

"What is going on in here?" boomed a loud voice, and Papa entered the barn. "You two boys stop fooling around. If there is any milk spilled because of your horseplay, you will both be taken behind the woodshed. Now, get your chores done. Your mom will have dinner done soon, and you both have homework."

The milk was poured into five-gallon cans and stored in the cold water of the spring house until the milk wagon came the next day to take the milk to the cheese factory several miles away. The family kept enough milk and cream for their immediate use and made butter for their bread. During the summer, ice cream was churned as a special treat. Any extra milk was given to the hogs.

The boys slipped into the house, hoping their father was cooled down from yelling at them in the barn. William whispered to

Daniel, "If we both go in and offer to help Mama, Papa will forget quickly that he was mad at us. You set the table, and I will offer to go back to the springhouse for a pitcher of milk."

"Why don't you set the table, and I will go to the springhouse for milk?" argued Daniel.

"Why don't you both go out and cut wood for your mother and let Abby set the table?" suggested Papa as he walked right up into their conversation without being noticed.

Running out the screen door, both boys headed for the woodpile and never looked back. Picking up the axes, the boys worked furiously until they heard their mama call them in for dinner. With sweat running into their eyes, and their shirts soaked from perspiration, the boys knew to wash up quickly before going to dinner.

Meekly entering the house, Mama kissed them both on the cheeks and thanked them profusely for all the chopped firewood. "That will last me for several days. That was so nice of you, boys." Sweetly, she led them to the table, and on their plates, both boys spied an extra piece of fresh bread spread thick with butter.

Looking at each other, a smile passed between them. Mama didn't know what Papa knew, and Papa would probably never tell on them. Abby just eyed the extra bread and was about to complain when she remembered Mama made her a special treat with cinnamon sugar. That was much better than buttered bread, and Abby sat back with a smug look on her face, determined to guard her special secret.

After dinner, Papa sent the boys out to gather the eggs. Abby stayed inside to help clear the dishes and dry them. The boys always said when Abby got older, she would need to take over gathering eggs. Fieldwork was too hard for the baby of the house, but collecting eggs were not.

Dad inspected the eggs when he buffed and placed carefully in the crate to be delivered to the general store. Between homemade butter, cream, and the eggs, Mama was able to trade for other items she could not grow on the farm. There were always bolts of cloth and thread needed to keep up with the growing children's needs for clothing the next size up.

Mama often sat in the living room nearest the most substantial source of light to mend clothes, while the boys struggled with their homework. Dad took the time to relax, smoke his pipe, and read a story to Abby. By the time the sun had set over the horizon, the children knew they better head to bed. Chores would come early again in the morning.

CHAPTER TWO

The boys would not be able to hitch a ride with Papa today even though he was going to deliver eggs, cream, and butter to the store. He had another errand that took him out of the house before breakfast.

"Mama, can we ride Jack to school today? He can carry us double for that distance. He will have a nice rest and lots of grass to graze on all afternoon while we are at school," Daniel asked.

"I don't see why not. Just make sure you hobble Jack so he can't runoff. You know he will run straight into the Mueller's cornfield and wreak havoc if you don't," Mama answered. "If you are going to saddle Jack, you better hurry."

Running off to the barn, Daniel was upset to see Jack was not in his stall. He assumed Papa turned the little horse loose when he hitched up the team. "Darn! William get some oats in that pail and shake it so Jack will hear. That is the only way we are going to get him to come back to us now that he is grazing. I'll get his halter and hide it, so he won't know we are about to catch him."

Will did as his older brother told him to do. Putting oats into the pail, he rattled it as he called, "Hey Jack…Ho there, Jack. Come on, Jack." William making smooching noises continued to coax the little dapple-gray pony closer as he held out the pail of oats.

Jack's ears pricked up, and he whinnied a greeting. His brain told him to run away, but his stomach told him to go investigate the oats. His nose twitched as he stepped closer to the boy. Finally, he closed the several steps to get his head in the pail and was happily munching away when Daniel slipped the rope around his neck and held it closed. Backing Jack away from the bucket, Daniel slid the halter over Jack's nose, ears, and poll and then strapped it tight at the cheek.

Nudging the pail, Jack demanded that he be allowed to finish the few scant grains at the bottom. Licking every last morsel, Jack finally allowed the boys to lead him back to the barn.

"I don't think we have time to saddle him, Daniel. We are going to be late for school if we don't leave right now."

William grabbed the bridle guiding the bit into Jack's mouth. He kept the halter on and passed the headstall over the ears and buckled it in place as well. William threw the reins up over Jack's back.

"We can ride bareback. We have done it many times before. Get on Daniel and pull me up behind you."

"Hold on to Jack while I get on. You know he will take off at a run if you don't hold him. He is such a brat!"

Scrambling onto the back of the pony, Daniel held the reins tightly while he reached down and pulled his brother up behind him. William was barely seated when Jack took off at full gallop. Kicking up dirt clods and gravel, the pony headed for the low hanging branch, hoping to unseat his riders. Daniel, having had that trick played on him before, pulled the right reins hard enough to make the pony swerve away from the danger of the branch. Realizing there was no choice, Jack settled down to a trot.

Getting to school just before the teacher rang the bell, the boys slid off Jack. "Where are the hobbles, William?

"I thought you brought the hobbles," William replied. "Just tie him to the rail and come on. Mama won't be happy if the teacher tells her we were late."

The boys were in their seats before the last chime of the bell. Looking around, Daniel noted everyone was in attendance today. The boys outnumbered the girls by two to one. Many of the farmers didn't feel their daughters needed education since they were just going to be married and raise children. However, more and more farmers were starting to feel their daughters should know how to read and write, too.

The little country school was a one-room building. Miss Turnbull was not very old. She was unusual in that she actually completed high school before she became the teacher. Some of the children heard she went to a year of college in the big city, but no one knew that for sure.

All the older boys had a crush on her. She was young and pretty; however, she was also very strict. She liked to make learning fun, but she would not tolerate any of her students goofing around or slacking off.

There were twenty students in all ranging in ages from five years of age to one older boy who was already eighteen years old. Oscar mooned over Miss Turnbull more than any of the other goofy boys. He asked Miss Turnbull if he could take her to the movie once, but Miss Turnbull told him matter-of-factly that she would never date one of her students and that he should not think of her in that way.

Most of the girls were very serious about learning. They knew their mothers never got a chance to go to school, and they were very fortunate. Even the smallest of the girls, Eloise, knew all her ABCs and could read fifty sight words.

When Miss Turnbull did not know an answer to a question that was asked of her, she promised she would have the response by the next week. That meant, Miss Turnbull would spend her day off at the town library researching whatever question was asked of her.

Miss Turnbull took a room with a widow lady who lived three miles away. She lived with Mrs. Granger throughout the school year, but during the summer break, Miss Turnbull would go back to the big city to find a job or to continue her own education. This was her third year of living with Mrs. Granger, and they became good friends.

Often, Mrs. Granger would pack cookies for the whole class or bake a sheet cake. Miss Turnbull wrote down every child's birthday, and Mrs. Granger made sure some special treat was sent in with Miss Turnbull on each birthday. If the child's birthday landed in the summer, Mrs. Granger would have an end-of-the-year birthday party for the summer birthdays.

The children in exchange would write thankyou letters, poems, and drew lovely pictures for Mrs. Granger to hang on her wall. One Saturday, all the children went to Mrs. Granger's house and helped her paint the outside of her home. It was the social party of the season, or so Miss Turnbull told the children. The children all turned out because they loved both Miss Turnbull and Mrs. Granger.

No one wanted to disappoint Miss Turnbull, especially Daniel and William. When the classroom heard the sputter and backfire of one of those new vehicles called an automobile chugging down the road, the boys looked at each other in fright, knowing what damage the excitable horse could cause. On this fateful day that the boys forgot to bring the hobble, no one was terribly surprised to hear Jack scream in fear and pull back with all his might, kicking and rearing as the fearsome vehicle came into sight. A loud crack could be heard as the wood splintered.

Running to the window, Jack cried, "Oh, no! Jack has just taken down the entire railing, and the horses are running free!"

All the children sprinted out the front door watching seven horses racing across the Mueller's cornfield away from the racket of the automobile. Miss Turnbull's horse, still hitched to her buggy, was racing behind the other seven, flattening row after row of corn.

"Catch the horses!" yelled Oscar, the oldest boy in the school, as he led the children in a race to the cornfields. Miss Turnbull stood looking at the damage the horses caused, and a look of shock and horror became etched on her pretty face. She didn't have the money to repay Mr. Mueller for the loss of the crops.

"Slow down, or we will spook the horses," Oscar said as he held up his hand to indicate the children should spread out and tiptoe towards the various horses now found munching happily on the ears of corn still on the stalks. The horse's fear of the chugging automobile long past was no longer a concern. The horses were only thinking of their stomachs. The corn was the main focus after the terrible fright.

William walked up to Jack and took his reins. He patted him soothingly on his neck and slowly turned him back in the direction of the school.

Daniel was maneuvering the horse and buggy, hoping to cause as little damage as possible to the field. Returning the way, the horse previously bolted was the only way to keep from plowing down more rows of cornstalks. Worried he and his brother would somehow be blamed since Jack was the first animal to react to the automobile, Daniel was trying hard to come up with a story to shift the blame.

'It wasn't Jack's fault he had never seen an automobile before...It was the driver of that automobile who should be blamed. He should make sure his stupid machine wasn't so noisy...Jack was only following the other horses....' Thoughts and excuses filled his head, but Daniel knew that he and his brother would be held responsible since they were supposed to have brought the hobble for Jack, who everyone knew was a nervous pony.

Miss Turnbull excused the class early and told them she needed to go and talk with Mr. Mueller about the destruction of part of his cornfield. Dread was on her face, and all the children were sad to see their teacher so upset. Slowly, the children gathered their belongings and walked out of the schoolhouse.

"Maybe we should go with her to talk to Mr. Mueller," said William to his brother. "She might need a witness to tell Mr. Mueller about the automobile and the havoc it caused. Besides, you know she is going to shoulder all the blame, and that isn't fair."

Daniel pulled William up onto Jack's back behind him. "Yeah, I think you are right. Miss Turnbull isn't to blame, and we need to make sure Mr. Mueller does not get mad at her. He does have a temper, but he is a fair-minded man, at least, that is what Papa says."

Following Miss Turnbull's buggy, the boys whispered scenarios that might follow, trying hard to think of excuses and plans to solve the problem. Upon entering the dirt drive to the Mueller farm, both boys became silent with apprehension.

Mr. Mueller, home for lunch, came out of his house with his wife on his heels. Visitors were rare out in the country, and it was always bad news, it seemed when anyone came to the door.

"Miss Turnbull, boys, what can I do for you? Tie up your horses and come on in. Mrs. Mueller has a pot of tea to share," Mr. Mueller said, hoping this was a social visit.

All three did as instructed and followed Mr. Mueller into the parlor of his home. Mrs. Mueller, indeed, did have cups of tea poured and waiting for the trio.

"I fear I have some bad news to share with you," said Miss Turnbull immediately, not waiting for any small talk to proceed. "My horse and buggy bolted through your cornfield and knocked down a row of cornstalks before it stopped."

"It wasn't her fault," William interjected immediately. "An automobile came down the road, and it scared all the horses. There was nothing Miss Turnbull could have done."

Daniel nodded his head emphatically to support what his brother had just said. Feeling a need to add one more thing, Daniel said, "I will help you when it is time to harvest your corn if that will help. I am big for my age and can just about keep up with the men."

Mr. Mueller, who never had born children, looked Daniel in the eyes. "That is very responsible of you. Your father will be proud of you. I might just take you up on your offer if it is alright with your father. I could use a hand at harvest time."

Turning his attention to Miss Turnbull, he softened his face. "I will go out and see how much damage was done. I suspect it will be less than what hail would cause. There are years that my whole crop is damaged due to drought, pests, or disease. I suspect a horse and buggy couldn't do that much damage. Thank you for owning up to what happened. That was very brave for such a young lady."

Not seeing the spark of temper that Mr. Mueller's reputation indicated made Daniel relax. He picked up his cup of tea and sipped. Miss Turnbull, too, relaxed and found herself chatting with Mrs. Mueller about lady-things.

Mr. Mueller got to his feet and asked Daniel and William to show him where the damage was done while he left his wife to chat with Miss Turnbull. Mr. Mueller knew how infrequently Mrs. Mueller got to gossip with a neighbor and how much she enjoyed those rare occasions.

The boys waited patiently in the yard as Mr. Mueller saddled his riding horse. They rode the short distance back to the little country school, talking about weather and crops. When they arrived, Mr. Mueller shook his head in disbelief. "How could one horse and buggy do so much damage?" he said under his breath.

Daniel and William knew better than to add any comment at this time. Neither wanted to tell that all the horses ran through the cornfield, but it would become apparent to Mr. Mueller as he walked his field.

"Well, a herd of deer could cause this much destruction in one night, so I guess it isn't as bad as I thought it might be," Mr. Mueller said out loud. "However, it isn't better than I hoped it might be either."

The boys shifted from foot to foot in nervousness. Neither wanted to tell the part Jack played in the havoc. William, ever honest, spoke up. "It wasn't Jack's fault. He got scared when the automobile came down the hill. He broke loose and ran away from the machine. I am afraid the other horses followed."

"I understand why you offered to help me harvest my cornfield. You are feeling guilty about Jack's role in what happened," Mr. Mueller said, "but you don't need to feel guilty. Jack wasn't the only horse to stampede, was he?"

"No, Sir," Daniel answered.

"Let's just forget your offer to help with the harvest. Your father is going to need your help at that time as well. It shows a good upbringing from your father that you offered to help. I have even more respect for your father now. He has raised good sons. I think you best get home."

Puffing with pride, Daniel said as he and William turned to mount Jack, "My offer still stands, Mr. Mueller. I do feel that I was responsible for some of the damage done to your crops. I would like to help any way I can."

Nodding a dismissal to the boys, Mr. Mueller proceeded further into the field as William and Daniel turned Jack towards home.

"What a nice man," said Daniel. "I always heard he was quick-tempered but fair. I can agree with the fair part of his personality. He was really fair to us."

"All I can say is I hope Papa is as fair. He is going to be mad at us when he hears what happened," William said over Daniel's shoulder. "I don't think we are going to get off so easy when he finds out we did not remember to take Jack's hobble when Mama told us to do so."

Once home, Jack was rubbed down and turned out to pasture. William and Daniel started on the chores immediately, hoping Papa would be impressed and not get mad at them when they retold the happenings of the day.

The boys were in trouble when they walked into the house for dinner. "Boys, why didn't you change into your work clothes when you got home from school? You know you only have two good pairs of jeans and three shirts for school. If you don't take care of them, what do you expect your mother to do? She already works harder than both of you put together. You think she has time to mend, wash, or make new shirts because you aren't responsible?" Papa scolded.

Both boys showed red coloring rising to their cheeks. Embarrassed that they forgot to change clothes when they got home, left them with no excuse except wanting to get in Papa's good graces before telling him the news from the day.

"What do you have to say to your mother? I think you owe her an apology and an explanation," Papa said, glaring at his two seated sons.

In unison, the two boys said, "We are sorry, Mama." William added, "We weren't thinking. Things got out of hand today."

Daniel wanted to kick his brother but knew the movement would be noticed by his father, and things would be worse. Instead, he jumped in and said, "It wasn't really our fault. It was the fault of the man who drove the automobile too fast down the road."

Papa didn't say a word. Staring hard from one boy to the other made Daniel squirmed under his father's intense gaze. "Let me start from the beginning, okay?"

Papa said, "That would be a good starting place."

"Well…" Daniel started, pausing to gather his thoughts. "Well, we were in class, and all the horses were tied to the porch rails as usual. Miss Turnbull was giving us directions for an assignment when we heard this horrendous noise coming down the road. It was an automobile, and it was chugging and making popping noises, and poor Jack ain't never seen or heard an automobile before, so he bolted. He took down the railing, and all the other horses ran, too. Miss Turnbull's horse, which was still hitched to the buggy, got scared as well, and it raced into Mr. Mueller's cornfield following all the rest of the horses." Again, Daniel paused and waited for his father's reaction.

"And…?" Papa asked without commenting on what Daniel had previously stated.

Continuing, Daniel said, "And there was quite a bit of damage done to Mr. Mueller's field. Miss Turnbull, William, and I went to Mr. Mueller's house to tell him what happened. Mr. Mueller, William, and I rode back to the school, so Mr. Mueller could see the damage to his field for himself."

"And…?" Papa questioned.

"And, I told Mr. Mueller I would help with harvesting his corn this year since Jack was the pony who led the stampede, but he said I was not at fault, so he does not expect me to help," Daniel said lowering his voice.

"Why was Jack tied to the railing?" Papa asked, knowing that Jack was an excitable pony and had torn down many hitching posts in the past.

"It was my fault, Papa," William said quickly. "I forgot Jack's hobble, and we didn't have another option."

"It was just as much my fault as Williams, Papa. I am the oldest. I should have made sure we took the hobbles, but we were running late for school since it took us so much time to catch Jack from the pasture."

Papa realized that he was partly to blame. He forgot the boys would need to ride Jack to school and turned him out to pasture. Relaxing his body language from the stern Papa to the kind, understanding Papa, Papa told the boys what would be happening. "It is my fault, too. I forgot you would need Jack to ride to school when I turned him out. I will tell you what we are going to do. First, tomorrow, all three of us are going to take new railings to the school and repair the damage done to the porch. Tomorrow is Saturday, so you won't be missing any schoolwork. Next, Daniel, you will help Mr. Mueller with his harvesting, as you promised. You will have double work, but there is no way around that since I will need both you boys to help me at the same time. On the weekends, William and I will help Mr. Mueller as well. Now, get ready for dinner. Change your clothes and wash up."

Both boys knew they dodged a bullet as they ran to their shared bedroom to change clothes. "I think that went well, don't you?" Daniel asked William.

William smiled. "It could have been a whole lot worse."

CHAPTER THREE

The next morning, after chores, Papa and the boys hitched the wagon and loaded it with all the tools necessary to repair the railings and porch at the schoolhouse. Before leaving, Papa showed Daniel and William how to make a temporary hobble out of rope. One could even use the reins of the bridle when unsnapped from the headstall.

"Watch closely, boys. This is not difficult, and I will expect you to use this technique if you ever forget Jack's hobble again. Fold the rope or rein in half and loop the rein around the front leg. Twist the remain rein or rope until there is the distance from your fist to your elbow of twisted rope and attach the other end to the loose foot. Tie it off by placing the one end of the free rope through and under the twisted rope and tie it off. There...it is done." Papa stepped back to show off his handiwork.

"One more thing that I don't think I should have to mention to you at your age, but obviously, I do. You never tie a horse up by the reins when the horse has a metal bit in its mouth. Jack could have broken his teeth by setting back as he did. You know you should have a halter on him even with his bridle. That way, you can tie him by his lead rope. I don't care if you will be late for school or not, do you understand? You will take the time necessary to do it right. Jack can't grow new teeth. Once they are broken, they are gone, and so will be his ability to eat well. You have the responsibility of taking good care of our animals. The horses are tools on this farm just like our plow or any other tool we need for our livelihood."

Beaming, Daniel said, "We did that one thing right, Papa. We left his halter on and tied him by the rope onto the rail. Jack's teeth are fine."

No more was said, and Papa knew the boys would never repeat the mistake of forgetting the hobble. He smiled, knowing there would be many other mistakes the boys would make in life. It seems learning never stops.

The wagon was hitched to Maud, who was healed, and Molly was waiting to be hitched up alongside Maud. The boys jumped up beside their father, and Papa clucked to the team to head out.

The damage was not as considerable as Papa feared. The boys helped hold the pieces of the railing as Papa hammered what could be salvaged back into place. New boards were used where the railing split into two separate parts. When the job was completed, Papa stepped back and looked at the project.

"Looks sturdy to me. What do you think, boys?"

Both boys nodded in agreement. Papa let his eyes stare at the damage done to Mr. Mueller's field. "I think we should stop over and talk to Mr. Mueller. I want to let him know you will be available to help with the harvest, and William and I will help on weekends as well. It is always good to help out one's neighbors even if you didn't cause the damage. One never knows when you might need a helping hand. You know the old saying, 'Do unto others,' right?"

Not staying long at the Mueller's farm, the boys got home early enough to enjoy some time off before the evening chores. Mama packed a picnic lunch, and the boys went down to the pond to fish.

"I wish Mama would let us go to the river to fish. I guess the boys who used to live here drowned in the river, and Mama is afraid we might, too. Someday, she is going to let us go to the river to fish. The bullheads and bluegill are muddy-tasting in this pond. If we can convince Mama how much better, the river fish would taste, and if we promise not to go into the river, maybe she will let us go. Northern Pike would sure taste good. Mama would not like eels if we caught them, though. She thinks they are ugly." Daniel laughed, picturing how his mother would react to the eels.

"Hey, I got something on my line. Get the net. I think it is big!" William yelled.

"Yeah, right," scoffed Daniel. "Anything big was fished out of here years ago. You will be lucky to catch a catfish weighing three pounds. We will need more than one fish to feed our family. Put that one on a stringer, and let's get serious about catching fish before we have to go home."

Putting a minnow on the hook, Daniel tossed his line straight out and into the water. Almost instantly, something from below captured the minnow and began tugging while rushing to his right.

"Whoopee! I've got a big one," Daniel yelled

"What is it?" asked William, excited for his big brother.

"I don't know. I can't see it. It keeps tugging my line underwater. This feels bigger than crappie." Daniel yelled as he battled the catch.

"Lift your pole. Bring it in," instructed William.

Nervously, Daniel yanked his pole straight up and flung the line back behind him, directly into William. William jumped up and down, screaming, "It's a snake! It's a snake!"

Scrambling to grab rocks, the boys pelted the aggressive water snake as it curled up and hissed at them with the minnow and hook still in its mouth. Realizing Daniel only had the one hook, the boys knew they would need to subdue the snake to retrieve the hook.

"Get that forked branch over there on the ground and hurry before the snake slithers away with my hook. I will try to keep its attention on me," Daniel yelled to Williams.

William quickly retrieved the branch and stuck the forked end just behind the snake's head and pressed down firmly to allow Daniel to pull the hook out of its mouth. Yanking the line from a distance to avoid a bite, Daniel was pleased to have the hook and minnow come free.

"That snake won't come anywhere near a minnow again," William said as the snake slithered away and back into the tall grass that grew down to the pond.

A few hours passed, and the boys became excited. The catfish started biting on worms. With crawfish and minnows as bait, as well as the worms, the boys had a good catch with five catfish, seven crappies, and one medium-sized bass to take home to their mama to cook for dinner.

Walking back home, the chatter begins. "You scared the bejeebers out of me when you threw that snake on me! I told you to pull it out, not yank it out," William said, laughing until tears were in his eyes. Daniel, belly laughed at the memory of William, prancing around like a little girl with the snake dangling from around his neck. Both boys were still laughing and coughing when they walked into the house.

"What's so funny?" Mama asked.

Not wanting to scare her into putting the pond out of bounds, Daniel said that William just farted.

"That's not funny," Mama said. "You are going to clean those fish for me outside. You know I don't like to clean fish, and they stink up the kitchen. I will cook them, but I am not cleaning them. Give the guts to the chickens and leave the fish head for your Papa to make it into fertilizer. You want me to fry them in cornmeal?" Mama said to the boys.

"Yes, Mama, cornmeal would be delicious," the boys said in unison and left the house with their catch to clean and a secret that both intended never to tell their mother about the snake.

Papa ate his fill of the fish. He told the boys it was the best fish he ever ate. Mama took that as a personal compliment to her cooking and beamed. Abby curled up her lips and scowled. She did not like fish at all, but it was the only thing on the table to eat besides vegetables and potatoes. Abby had one tiny piece of fish and mainly potatoes on her plate. Mama scowled at her daughter.

"Abby, you need to learn to like fish. We aren't always going to eat pork, beef, or chicken. Fish is good for you, so take more than that one small piece...." Noticing Abby's defiant face, Mama added, "or you can sit at the table until you do!"

Mama reached and put another small piece of fish onto Abby's plate. Abby slouched down in her chair and folded her arms across her chest. Everyone knew this was going to be a very long evening since Abby could be as stubborn as a mule.

The boys immediately got up from the table and cleared everything except Abby's plate. Daniel knew from past experiences that Mama would not back down until it was bedtime, and then she would send Abby straight to bed. Papa always stayed out of the battle.

"Thank you, boys, for clearing the table. I know you have a few chores yet to do, so you are excused. Your sister will just sit at the table until she can do as she was told," Mama said with a sideways glance at her determined daughter.

With water heating on the stove to wash the dishes, Mama's back was turned from the table. Daniel, feeling sorry for his little sister, quietly tip-toed over to her chair and bent down and whispered to her.

A big smile crossed Abby's face, and she immediately sat up and started to eat her food. Daniel left the house with William in tow.

Once outside, William asked, "What did you say to Abby to make her eat her dinner?"

"I told her we would take her with us the next time we went fishing," Daniel replied.

"But Mama is not going to let her go fishing with us. She is only four years old and a girl at that," William sneered.

"You know darned well that we can sneak off and fish anytime we want, and Abby will never know. I am not stupid enough to actually take her, but she doesn't know that," laughed Daniel.

"That isn't even nice, Daniel. In fact, that is rather mean of you," William said, actually feeling bad for the trick Daniel just played on their little sister.

Once chores were finished, the boys came back into the house and played a card game. The family had little extra money for games and toys, but a deck of cards cost very little, so Papa brought home a pack last year at Christmas for the family. Papa had said, "There are many games you can play with cards. I will teach you a few, and later when you are older, I will teach you several more."

At this point, the boys knew how to play *Go Fish, War, Spoons,* and *Rummy.* Playing *War,* the boys were delighted when Papa said the whole family should play a game and suggested *Spoons.* Racing to the table, William got out four spoons and neatly made a circle in the center of the table with the spoons, waiting for the family to gather. Daniel came with the deck of cards and shuffled them until everyone was seated. Papa reviewed the rules of the game for Abby.

"I will be the dealer this time. I will deal-out four cards to each of you. The object, Abby, is to make four of a kind in your hand," Papa said directly to his little daughter. "I will take the top card from the pile, and I will decide if I want to keep it or get rid of one of the cards in my hand. I will pass the one I don't want to my left, face down, and so will everyone else with the last person discarding the one they do not want on the discard pile face down. Quickly, another card is drawn by the dealer into his hand, and then everyone passes a card to their left until someone has four of a kind in their hand. Once someone has four of a kind, they grab a spoon, and a mad scramble follows as everyone else tries to grab a remaining spoon. The person who has four of a kind can try to be sneaky and grab a spoon when no one notices. Do you remember how to play, Abby?"

Letting Abby sit on her knees so she could reach the spoons, the family started the game. The cards flew wildly around the table until Mama grabbed a spoon, and everyone followed suit, leaving Papa without a spoon.

"I guess I have an *S*, this time, but I am not going to be the one who spells *Spoon* first," Papa said, rubbing his hand where his knuckles were smacked in the free-for-all.

The game went on with laughter and occasional sore hands, but everyone was having fun until Mama started to rub her back. "I'm sorry, kids, but I need to lie down. My back is really hurting."

Mama got up from the table, and Papa wore a worried look on his face. Mama was due to have the new baby any day. Papa wondered if Mama's back pain was an indication that the baby would be born tonight.

"Please, take one spoon off the table and continue to play. I was close to having spoon spelled out anyway," Mama said as she pushed her chair under the table. Papa's eyes followed her as she went into their small bedroom and closed the door.

"Children, you know Mama is due to have the baby very soon. When she has the baby, we are all going to need to chip in and do more for her. Sometimes, we are all going to have extra chores, including holding the baby while Mama cooks. Daniel, you are old enough to do some of the cooking as well. There are a few recipes that are easy that you can cook. For a while, Mama will need extra help. I expect all of you to help without complaining. We are a family, and family helps out each other." Papa shuffled and dealt the cards as he gave the pep talk to the children.

The next morning there was no new baby. It was Sunday, and Mama said she would not be going to church that day. Papa thought everyone should skip church and stay home with Mama, but Mama said no to that.

"Church is important. Our children need to learn about God. I will not have them skip church because of me," Mama said. "No, you will take them all to Sunday school and church. Ask Mrs. Jurgens if she would mind stopping over after church."

Papa knew Mrs. Jurgens was the mid-wife. That meant Mama was expecting to have the baby today.

With the children dressed in their Sunday best, Papa hitched the wagon, and the family left Mama in the house alone. When the family arrived at the church without Mama, several knowing glances were seen amongst the women. Mrs. Jurgens excused herself from the church service and took her buggy and left to help Mama.

"We will drop you off at your house after church," Papa said to Mr. Jurgens. "I feel much better knowing Mrs. Jurgens is with my wife."

Papa did not listen to a word the pastor said during the sermon. His mind was on Mama. He constantly prayed for the safe arrival of the new baby during the service.

Church service often seemed long to Papa, who never went to church before he met Mama, but today it seemed eternally long. When church service was over, and Mr. Jurgens was finished talking with friends, everyone got onto the wagon and headed to Mr. Jurgen's house.

Mr. Jurgens seemed to understand Papa's impatience for him to get off the wagon. He smiled knowingly at Papa and said, "Everything will be fine. My Helen is a fine mid-wife. Don't worry so much. Having babies is a natural thing. Your wife will be fine, and soon you will be the proud Papa of another fine boy or beautiful little girl." Thanking Papa for the ride, Mr. Jurgens finally left and went inside.

Papa snapped the reins across the back of the team to send them off at a trot. Arriving home, Papa gave Daniel the reins and told him and William to take care of unhitching the team and rubbing down the horses. Reaching up for Abby, he went into the house to see how Mama was doing.

The boys drove the wagon to the barn and unhitched the horses as told. William seemed nervous as he rubbed down Molly. Sensing his anxiety, Molly side-stepped and fidgeted while William worked.

"Knock it off, William. You are spooking Molly. Slow down with the brushing and stroke her. You being a Nervous Nelly is not going to help Mama at all. You heard Mr. Jurgens. Giving birth is natural. Mama is going to be fine," Daniel said.

"But Daniel, remember when our cow, Clara, gave birth and we lost the calf? Sometimes things go wrong. What if something goes wrong with Mama?" William countered.

Daniel finished currying Maud and led her out of the barn and through the gate to the pasture. Coming back, he took the brush from his little brother. "Go to the house and see for yourself. Mama is fine. Stop thinking so negatively."

William ran from the barn, and Daniel continued to brush Molly until she shined. Knowing Molly would immediately roll in the grass after being turned out did not stop Daniel from doing his best work. Daniel was in no rush to meet his new sibling. It only meant more work for him to have a baby around.

William met Mrs. Jurgens as she was leaving the house. Her team was hitched in the shade of the big oak tree. William knew by the look on Mrs. Jurgens' face that his mama was fine.

"Congratulations, William. You are now the big brother to a fine, strapping baby boy. I forgot to ask your mama what she was going to name her new son. Do you know by any chance?" Mrs. Jurgens asked as she got up onto the seat of the wagon.

William just stammered. He remembered several names being considered, but he was at a loss as to which one they decided upon. "I am sorry, Mrs. Jurgens. I don't remember if it is going to be Wilbur or Clarence. I can run into the house and find out and come right back and tell you."

"No worries, William. I will find out his name at the baptism at church. I can wait until then." Smiling, Mrs. Jurgens drove her wagon out of the lane and onto the road, heading back to town.

William did not wait for the wagon to leave the lane. He continued his quick step into the house. Finding Mama holding the new baby, he smiled when Mama told him to come over and meet his newest brother.

William sat on the arm of the sofa and looked down on the wrinkled, red face of his new brother and thought that he was very ugly. "Mama, why couldn't we get a cute brother?"

Mama laughed. "He is cute. All babies look like this after they are born. You were so fat, your eyes were like little slits in your face, but look at you now. You are so handsome you take my breath away. Your little brother will be handsome, too. Just wait and see."

"Mama, I forgot what you and Papa decided to name him," William said, feeling sheepish that he paid so little attention when names were being picked out.

Papa answered the question. He was sitting next to Mama with his arm around her shoulder. "This strong, young man will be named for my Uncle George. William, meet your brother, George."

"George?" came a voice from the opened door. "I thought you had decided on Clancy," Daniel said as he entered the house.

"That was your mama's choice, but we drew straws, and she got the short one, so George it is," Papa said, laughing at his wife, who acted as if she lost the biggest battle of her life when George became the name.

"The next boy will be Clancy, and I won't be drawing straws!" Mama said in pretend indignation.

Abby, quiet until now, said, "Mama, can I hold the baby?"

A worried look crossed Mama's face, but it vanished as Papa got up so Abby could take his place on the small sofa. Mama passed the swaddled baby to Abby giving her instructions to support the baby's head at all times.

Abby cooed and smiled at her little brother. "You are no longer the baby of this family, Abby. How does it feel to be the big sister?" Papa asked.

"I love my baby brother. I am going to be the best big sister in the whole wide world. " Abby continued to gaze down at the baby with adoration in her eyes.

Mama beamed. "I know you are going to be my best helper. I am certainly glad you are here to help, Abby. I don't think I could handle one more child without you."

"Hey!" interjected William. "I can be a big helper, too."

"I am counting on your help, William and your help, too, Daniel. I know you will all pitch in and help me out with the new baby."

"I ain't changing diapers!" Daniel said defiantly.

"Only when I really need you to do so, Daniel. I know that you will have extra chores outside when I need William to help me with the baby...." Mama said this with a twinkle in her eye, knowing Daniel would make the connection at some point that it might be easier to rock a baby than muck out stalls.

CHAPTER FOUR

The months went past quickly with the added chores in the house. Everyone helped out with the new baby as their schedules allowed. Daniel did have more outside tasks than before, but he rarely complained. He really did not like sitting quietly while holding the baby. He preferred to be working and moving around. Sitting still just was not his style. That is one reason school and church were not his favorite places to be. He would much prefer to be riding, hunting, or fishing.

William being a quieter boy, enjoyed the moments he got to sit in the rocker and hold his little brother while Mama made dinner. Getting out of the hard work of milking cows or feeding animals was a treat. School, for William, was the best time of the day. He loved sitting, reading, and learning new things.

Abby was allowed to hold the baby as long as she was sitting down. Mama still did not trust her to carry the baby even to his cradle. However, during the day when the boys and Papa were gone, even Abby just sitting with the baby and singing songs was helpful for Mama.

Mama still had all the chores of baking, cooking cleaning, laundry, sewing, and mending. Mama often teased Papa with the old saying that 'Men work from sun to sun, but women's work is never done.' Papa only grunted and asked Mama if she would like to change places and work in the hot field all day long. Mama, in reply, would ask Papa if he would like to give birth to their next child. The banter usually stopped with that remark.

Papa slaughtered one of the hogs and smoked it to give to the Jurgens in exchange for Mrs. Jurgen's help with Mama and the birth of baby George. Money never changed hands when an exchange of goods would work as well. A farmer needed every cent he had, to keep the farm productive. City people, like the Jurgens, were happy getting fresh meat, which cost a lot of money in the store, so each was happy in the trade.

One particular Saturday, Papa carried extra eggs and butter to the store. Mama had a long list of items she needed but could not ride along with Papa since baby George was colicky. Papa asked the boys if they would like to ride along since the morning chores were completed.

The boys ran to wash up and change clothes. Any chance to go to town was a treat. William was thinking of penny candy, and Daniel was hoping to get a glance at Ellie, a cute blue-eyed girl with shiny auburn hair that he knew from church. Daniel took extra time putting pomade in his hair to keep it in place just in case Ellie might be at the store. Ellie's Papa owned the general store, and often on Saturdays, Ellie would help out.

Papa hollered and said he was leaving with or without the boys. A mad race followed as the boys flew out the screen door and to the waiting wagon. Papa asked Daniel if he wanted to drive the team.

"Yes, Papa," Daniel answered. "I would love to drive."

Moving the team out at a faster pace than Papa would have done, Papa reprimanded Daniel. "Slow down! We have eggs in the back, and I don't want a single one cracked. What's your hurry, anyway?"

William giggled, "Ellie is the hurry, Papa. Daniel has a crush on her, and she might be working at the store today."

Papa only smiled. "Slow down. We will be staying the same amount of time whether you rush or not."

Daniel pulled back gently on the reins to slow the forward movement of the team. Back to a steady walk, the horses' click-clop cadence lulled William to sleep in the back of the wagon, where he stretched out to watch the clouds floating past in the warm sky. Before falling asleep, William pointed up to the sky and said, "That cloud looks like Shep, and that one over there looks like Abby's Teddy Bear." Soon not a peep was heard from William as he dozed off.

"That cloud does look like a Teddy Bear," said Papa. "And that one looks like a dragon."

"Dragon? There is no such thing as a dragon, Papa," Daniel said, never having much of an imagination.

"Oh, come on, Daniel. Use your imagination. You have heard stories of knights fighting dragons. There must have been some creature that inspired those stories. Maybe it was not a fire-breathing dragon-like the stories say, but it could have been one of those Komodo dragons I have read about. The books say one bite from that reptile could kill a bull."

"Really, Papa?" Daniel said, genuinely amazed. "I wouldn't want to fight a creature that could kill a bull with one bite. Do we have Komodo dragons here?"

"No, Daniel, we don't. They are overseas somewhere. I guess in a country called Komodo. The worst thing we have here are rattlesnakes, and I have warned you to be on the lookout for them all the time. We had one in the haybarn last year if you remember. Luckily, I saw it first and killed it. But...I want you to remember, even though they aren't under every rock, you need to act as if one might be."

"I heard Oscar say his great uncle was killed by a rattlesnake. Oscar wasn't born yet, but his mother still talks about it. It is almost like Mama talking about the boys who used to live on our farm drowning in the river. That reminds me," Daniel said, "when can William and I fish in the river. The fish taste better out of the river than in our muddy old pond."

"I will take you and William to the river tomorrow after church if your mother thinks she can handle Abby and the baby by herself for a couple of hours. If I am along, I know she will let you boys go, especially if she does not have to clean the fish."

Reaching town, William woke up as the team came to a stop with the lulling, rocking movement of the wagon ceasing. Yawning and stretching, suddenly, William got to his feet and fidgeted from foot to foot.

William said nervously, "I really need to pee."

"William, you know your mother doesn't like you to use that word. She says it is crude. You are supposed to say you need to relieve yourself. Go ahead and use the privy around the back of the store and meet us inside."

William jumped off the wagon and raced down the alley to the back of the store where the outhouse could be found, leaving Daniel to help his father unload the goods.

Daniel said grudgingly, "I bet he didn't really have to go. He just wanted to get out of work. William is getting soft ever since the baby arrived. He does very little work outdoors, and his muscles are getting puny."

Papa just grunted as he put another box of eggs on top of the carton Daniel was holding. "Be careful when you go up the steps to the store. I wouldn't want you to drop the eggs now that we are this close to getting them inside."

With both arms loaded with cartons, Daniel was especially thankful when someone opened the door to the store for him. Seeing it was Ellie, Daniel almost dropped the containers.

"Hello, Daniel," said a soft voice behind the pretty smiling lips of the most beautiful girl in the whole town.

Daniel just stood in the open doorway, gawking at the pretty girl with the sparkling blue eyes. Papa gave Daniel a gentle shove from behind since his arms were also loaded down with boxes.

"Daniel, move on to the counter. I need to put down my boxes of butter. They are heavier than your eggs, and I want to set them down NOW." The last word was said with enough emphasis that Daniel was startled out of his mooning for Ellie.

"Ellie, could you help Mrs. Strickland to find the ribbon she needs for her dress?" Ellie's father said as Papa and Daniel made their way to the counter.

Papa and the storekeeper talked for several minutes, and a handshake was given along with the list from Mama. Daniel stood and watched Ellie until William came into the store and gave Daniel the *gag me* sign where he put his finger down his throat while pretending to wretch. That embarrassed Daniel enough that he let his eyes leave Ellie.

While William looked at the jars of penny candy, deciding which one he would get when Papa asked him to make his selection, Daniel watched as two boys from town came into the store with a box with several holes cut out. Wondering what could be in the box, Daniel moved closer to eavesdrop.

"How much for twenty pigeons, Mr. Cook?" asked one of the boys.

"Let me see. I can get twenty to thirty cents for each squab, but I can't pay you that much, or I won't make a profit. What if I pay you fifteen cents per pigeon or dove if it weighs one pound and is still young and tender?" Mr. Cook replied.

Moving excitedly towards William, Daniel told his brother what he just heard. "Just think of all that money waiting for us to collect in the barn and other outbuildings. I bet we have several dollars' worth of pigeons and doves out in the buildings. All we have to do is net them, bring them in, and we will have money to spend on ourselves. You could buy all the penny candy in the store!"

Thinking about all the penny candy he would be able to buy, William said he was willing to climb into the rafters to catch the pigeons. "We have a net, and if we go at night when the birds are asleep, we could probably get them all at one time."

"I was thinking the same thing. I don't think we need to tell Mama or Papa. Mama would say it is too dangerous, and then Papa would tell us we can't climb the rafters. I say we go out tonight after everyone is asleep. What do you say?" Daniel said in a conspiratorial whisper.

William was so excited; he was heading out the door to the wagon when his father called him back to see if he wanted some candy. Rushing back to the counter, William selected the jawbreaker, knowing it would last most of the trip home. Daniel opted for bubble gum. He claimed it would last for days if his mother did not make him throw it away.

Unpacking the groceries and goods was the first priority once they arrived home. Abby rushed into her father's waiting arms to see which pocket would hold her candy surprise. It was a game they started when she was barely old enough to eat candy, and it was still a favorite game for Papa.

With chores finished, dinner eaten, dishes washed, and dried, the family sat together in the small living room while Papa played his fiddle. Papa said he needed to practice for the barn dance that would be held in two weeks. Feeling fun-loving, the boys danced around the room, locking arms and kicking up their heels. Abby laughed and demand to dance with the boys until Mama finally said the children were getting too rough. She feared some of her furniture would get broken.

Baby George seemed to be able to sleep through anything. Mama held him in her arms as she kept time to the music with her toe-tapping. Mama said she would probably need to miss this barn dance since George was too small to bring along, but the family knew they would be able to convince her to come if not to dance, then to socialize.

Papa finally said he was tired, and everyone should get ready for bed. The two boys scampered off to their second-floor bedroom without complaint. They both knew the sooner everyone was asleep, the sooner they could sneak out and catch pigeons and doves.

When the house seemed quiet, Daniel needed to nudge William from his sleep. He mumbled something about *the spirit being willing but the flesh being weak,* quoting something he read in one of his many books borrowed from the library or maybe something Mama read from the Bible. Daniel didn't care to find out more since he was in a hurry to get to the barn.

Quietly tip-toeing down the stairs, the boys opened the door and softly let it close as they slipped out, Daniel thinking to grab the lantern style flashlight setting by the door. Shep, who slept on the porch, opened his eyes and yawned, but did not bark. He got to his feet, tail wagging, and followed the boys happily into the night.

The barn door creaked as it was drawn open enough to allow the boys and Shep inside. Stomping could be heard from the stalls as the horses sniffed the air to see who the intruders might be. A soft nicker was heard from Jack, who immediately recognized the boys and hoped for some extra oats.

Daniel flicked on the lantern and nodded towards the ladder leading to the hayloft. "We can go up into the loft and catch a few up there. After that, I guess we will have to shimmy along the rafter to catch the other birds."

The first few were easy to catch with the net as they slept in the hayloft. Having the good sense to have a crate available before the end of their workday, Daniel dragged it up the ladder to keep the pigeons contained. Noting the older boys in town punched holes in their box for air, Daniel duplicated their efforts by punching holes into the wooden crate earlier that afternoon.

William was quiet and fast. He scooped up five birds without waking many. The flutter of wings told Daniel that a few pigeons flew further away but lighted again on the rafters. He knew if they kept the light soft, they would have a good chance to catch most of the birds in the barn in one night.

"William, I have room for several more pigeons in the crate. I will give you a boost up onto the rafter, and I want you to shimmy along the rafter until you can reach a bird," Daniel suggested.

"Okay, but how am I going to hand the birds back to you so you can put them in the crate. Once I get halfway along the rafter, I won't be able to reach you," William said.

"Of course, you will. That net has a long pole. You won't have to go all the way to the middle to catch most of them. Just net one, pass the pole back to me, and I will put the bird in the crate. I will pass the net back to you, and you can net the next one. If you get to the point where you can't pass the pole back to me, we will quit for the night and come up with another plan," Daniel said.

William sat with his legs dangling on either side of the beam and scooched along the rough wooden rafter with the pole tucked under his arm. Seeing a pigeon sleeping with its head tucked under its wing, William reached out and swiped it off the beam into his net. Excited, but not wanting to wake the sleeping birds, William whispered back to his brother, "I got it. Now, can you reach it?"

Daniel extended his arm and stretched enough to grab the net with the trapped bird inside. Putting the bird into the crate without allowing any of the trapped birds to escape, Daniel handed the net back to his brother.

William scooted a little further and was equally successful catching the next two birds on the rafter since they were sitting so close together that there was not even a finger space between them.

"Two with one netting!" snickered William, "I am getting good at this."

"Don't get too cocky. We still have about seven birds that I can see. Hand me the two you just caught," Daniel whispered loudly.

William moved several inches further to catch the two pigeons, and now he found he was out of reach to hand the netted birds back to his brother. "I am going to need to lean backward to pass the birds to you."

"Just reach a bit further. I think I can still hand over the net of pigeons if you stretch out your arm towards me," Daniel advised.

Sitting up on the rafter, William leaned back as far as he could without falling. "I can almost reach it, William. Just stretch your arm back another two inches, and I can get it," Daniel said as he strained as far over the loft as possible while still holding on to a support post.

William leaned back two more inches, and just as Daniel got hold of the net, William found himself off-balance and teetering on the rafter. With nothing to hold onto, William yelled as he fell from the beam to the barn floor below.

"Oh, no! Oh, no!" Daniel said as he dropped the netted birds and ran for the ladder.

William lying on the ground was crying in pain. Reaching his brother quickly, Daniel leaned over William, asking him what hurt.

"It's my leg. It hurts something fierce," William said through clutched teeth. "I think I broke it."

"I will help you up, and you can lean on me. We can get you back to the house," Daniel said, hoping his younger brother was only scared and not seriously hurt.

Screaming in pain as Daniel tugged on William's arm trying to get him to his feet, William turned ashen and yelled, "No! Don't move me again, or I am going to vomit. Go get Papa."

Daniel hesitated, knowing Papa was going to be really mad at him for allowing his little brother on the rafter. Hearing William whimpering, Daniel raced for the barn door and was halfway to the house before Shep even knew he was gone.

Shep, our dog, took two steps to give chase, but immediately turned and looked at William lying on the barn floor. Walking back to William, Shep licked William's face and laid down next to the boy to comfort and protect him.

Running through the dark yard, Daniel tripped twice, having left the lantern in the barn for William. Stumbling into the house, Daniel called out to Papa, waking baby George in the process.

Mama woke first, never sleeping deeply due to the needs of the new baby. Bolting straight up, hearing the urgency in Daniel's voice, she poked her husband from his sleep while slipping from the bed.

"Harlan, wake up! Something is wrong!" Lenora said to her husband while rushing to the living room.

Papa waking quickly, moved through the now opened door to his son. "Daniel, what are you doing up and fully dressed at this hour?"

"Papa, William broke his leg. He is out in the barn." Daniel said without giving any explanation as to why he and his brother were not sound asleep as they were supposed to be at that time of the night.

"Lenora, get me two stout pieces of wood from the woodpile and a roll of bandages. Daniel, you stay here and wait for your mother to give you the items I need and then bring them to me as quickly as you can," Papa said while pulling on his trousers and shoes.

Mama moved to find the items Papa would need and shouted for Daniel to pick up the baby and rock him, so he did not wake Abby. Daniel did as his mother said without saying his usual sass, 'That's woman's work.' Daniel knew better than to add to the trouble he was already in.

Mama returned shortly with the roll of bandages and two long pieces of wood. She knew precisely what Papa needed to splint William's leg. Wanting nothing more than to run out to see how her son was fairing, but knowing the baby needed her attention to calm him back to sleep, Mama gave the items to Daniel and said, "Go! Papa needs these."

Giving the baby to Mama, Daniel grabbed the roll of bandages and the two splints and rushed out the door into the dark. He found his Papa kneeling beside William. William's pant leg was rolled up to the knee as Papa evaluated the injury.

Soothingly, Papa said, "There, there, William. It is not as bad as it could be, but we will need to splint the leg and get you to the Mennonite hospital in town."

Taking the splints and the roll of bandages from Daniel, Papa barked an order to his eldest son. "Daniel, hitch up the wagon. We need to take your brother into town to have his leg set. Oh, and get something soft for your brother to lie upon as well. Those feed bags will do nicely for now. I will need you to go and get a comforter to cover your brother as well... Go! Hurry!"

When Daniel finished hitching the team to the wagon and made a soft place for his brother to lie down in the bed behind the seat, he ran to the house to retrieve the patchwork comforter Mama made two winters ago. He wanted to make his brother comfortable.

Racing up the stairs to get the comforter, Daniel answered his mother's question as he took the steps two at a time. "Yes, Mama, William is going to be fine. Papa said it wasn't as bad as he thought it might be."

Coming down the stairs, Daniel added, "We are taking William to the hospital in town so the doctor can set his bones."

"Oh my..." Mama said. "Tell Papa to drive carefully. Those roads are so rutted. It is going to be painful for your brother."

Daniel could hear the concern in his mother's voice and knew he was to blame for the whole mess. William could be sound asleep in bed if it was not for his hare-brained scheme to make a little spending money. Now, every cent would need to go to pay the doctor and hospital for William's care. Daniel knew there was no extra money lying around the house for doctors. Every cent was tied up in the farm.

Returning to the wagon, Daniel found Papa had lifted William into the back. "Daniel, you will need to drive the team. I am going to stay in the back with William to try to comfort him as best as I can. Hand me the comforter and get up on the seat," Papa said.

Daniel took the reins and clicked for the team to move out of the yard and onto the road. The lantern was brought along, but Daniel and Papa both knew it would not last the whole trip. Luckily, the horses had good eye-sight in the dark, and Daniel knew the road well.

Keeping the team to the center of the road, Daniel tried to stay out of the ruts previously made by wagons when the roads were wet from the rain. The grooves could be deep, and the jostling of the wagon proved to be as painful as Mama predicted it would be for William.

William was sweating and crying out with each drop of the wheel as one would fall into the deep groove of the dirt road. Daniel maneuvered the team as skillfully as possible for a young boy with limited experience driving a wagon. Luckily, Daniel, being the eldest son, had driven a wagon much more than most boys his age and proved to be almost as skillful as a grown man.

What seemed like days but was only two and a half hours before the wagon arrived at the entrance to the hospital. Mama telephoned ahead on the party line to make sure the doctor would be available to meet the wagon.

Doc Whitney greeted Papa, as the gurney with two muscular young orderlies came to assist William out of the back of the wagon. Being as gentle as possible, William still cried out in pain through clutched teeth. Daniel winced with each cry, feeling guilt and sympathy with each sound uttered by his brother.

"Why don't you and your son have a seat in the waiting room while I see just how badly this young man has fractured his leg. It looks like you have done a good job with your first aid splinting. I doubt that wagon ride did much good, though," Doc Whitney said as he guided Papa and Daniel to an area where they could wait.

Papa said, "Daniel did a good job avoiding most of the bad ruts in the road. I doubt I could have done any better."

Daniel swelled with pride at his father's praise, but only momentarily. Once Doc Whitney was gone, Papa turned his intense eyes to his son. "Now, young man, what were you and your brother doing in the barn in the middle of the night?"

"Daniel let his eyes lock with his father's eyes and knew he needed to tell the truth immediately with no hemming and hawing. Papa was not going to be put off even one more second.

Without hesitation, Daniel told his father the story. "It was all my fault, Papa. When we were at the store the other day, some older boys brought in pigeons and doves to sell to the storekeeper. They were getting fifteen cents per bird. I thought William and I could make some money since we knew there were lots of pigeons and doves in the outbuildings. I knew the birds would be asleep at night and easy pickings. With William being the lighter of the two of us, we decided he should be the one to go up on the rafters to net the sleeping birds and well…he fell."

"What were you thinking? Your brother could have broken his neck. It is bad enough that he broke his leg. You know doctors and hospitals cost a whole lot of money. Where do you think we are going to get the money to pay for all this? Those pigeons you just caught are not going to help much to pay for the bill. I will need to use the money I saved, hoping to buy a tractor." Papa said the last words to himself, not really meaning them for Daniel, but knowing what would need to be done.

"Papa, I can work after school to help pay for the hospital bills," Daniel spoke up.

"You are going to need to do your chores and your brother's chores until William is healed. I don't see how you can work anywhere else," Papa said, squelching Daniel's idea.

Daniel, feeling downcast, did not reply. He sat thinking how he could possibly contribute to paying off the bill when Doc Whitney came into the room.

"All done. William won't be in much pain on the ride home. I gave him a mild sedative of morphine and scopolamine to set his leg, and he is still drowsy from the injection. His cast is almost dry, so you should be able to leave in a short time," Doc Whitney said. Continuing, the doctor added, "A bill will be sent to the home. I am sure you can make arrangements in the billing office to make payments. It won't be as much as it would have been if the fracture was a compound fracture. Luckily for William, it was a clean break that required nothing more than setting the bone and casting it. He will need to be off that leg for a week or two, and then, he can use crutches to get around, but without putting weight on the leg until I see him again in six weeks. You can probably buy the crutches here at the hospital, but I know if you ask around, there will be someone in town who has a pair you can buy for cheaper or maybe even borrow them. Most of the townsfolk are good about helping. You might even ask your pastor if he knows someone who has crutches you can use."

Papa and Doc Whitney shook hands, and Papa told him how grateful he was for the excellent care the doctor had given his boy. The doctor left knowing he had little time to sleep before returning in the morning to complete his rounds of the hospital and then see patients in his office. Being disturbed at night was just one of the drawbacks of being one of the only doctors in town.

William was loaded on the back of the wagon once the cast was dry. He was dozing and barely aware of any movement. Papa decided Daniel could stay in the back with his brother as he drove the team home. Other than an occasional whimper, William stayed asleep for the entire ride home.

Mama was thrilled to see William. He opened his eyes and smiled at his mama, and that caused both joy and relief to spread across her pretty face.

"Doc Whitney says William will be just fine in six to eight weeks. Doc does not want William to put weight on his leg for several weeks, so I will need to buy or borrow some crutches. Right now, William needs to stay off his feet." Papa relayed the instructions to Mama as she listened intently.

Mama quickly said, after a moment's thought. "Deloris and Hiram's boy broke his leg a few years ago. They may still have the crutches he used. If you are going to church today, you can ask to borrow them."

Papa looked gloomily back to his wife. "I thought I would skip church today. I have been up all night, and I could use a nap. Besides, the team has made a long trip already. I don't think it is fair to hitch them up again. Daniel is rubbing them down, feeding them, and turning them out to pasture as we speak."

"I will phone her on the party line after church this afternoon to see if they have them. I guess William won't need them for a couple of weeks anyway."

Mama made up a bed on the sofa for William so she could keep an eye on him during the day. She bent down and gave his forehead a light kiss.

"William feels a little warm to me. Did Doc say we would need to be concerned about infection?" Mama asked as she turned towards the kitchen to start breakfast.

Papa followed her into the largest room in the house. He bent down and put wood into the stove to help Mama. Papa really wanted some coffee. Without the stovetop getting hot, there would be little chance for a cup of hot coffee soon.

Busily helping out, Papa said, "Doc said the break was clean and not a compound fracture, so he doesn't think there should be any infection. I think William is just warm from Daniel keeping the comforter up around his neck for the whole ride home. It wasn't all that cold outside. I think we are going to have an early summer this year and probably a hot one judging by the weather this spring.

Mama was mixing up a batch of pancakes when Daniel came into the house. He was feeling sheepish, not knowing if Mama was mad at him for causing William's broken leg.

"Daniel, breakfast is just about ready. You can wait with milking the cows until after you have eaten," Mama called out.

"What can I do to help, Mama?" Daniel asked in a quiet voice, not wanting to wake his sleeping brother.

Looking at the sofa, Daniel noticed William was still sound asleep. The patchwork comforter was thrown over him, and Daniel let his eyes look at each colorful patch, realizing many of the pieces were from old clothes he and his siblings had worn out. Daniel also saw one patch that was from Mama's past Sunday best dress that she outgrew after putting on a few pounds. Daniel remembered it was her favorite dress, and Mama said she could not part with it, so it would become something she could keep forever.

The memories flooded back into Daniel's mind as he recalled Abby wearing a little yellow dress with small blue cornflowers printed evenly across the yellow background. Mama called Abby *Sunshine* whenever she wore that dress. She really teared up when cutting the dress into squares for the comforter. Mama said it was ruined when Abby tore a large hole into the dress in the front. It did not take her long the sew the colorful squares into the comforter. Daniel admitted the material livened up the quilt and made it much cheerier. Much of the comforter was made from squares of the boys' clothes, which were darker in color.

Mama interrupted Daniel's thoughts by asking him to set the table and then to wake Abby, who slept soundly through the whole night, even with all the happenings that occurred.

Daniel almost raced to the kitchen when his mother asked for help. He was still waiting for her scolding. He knew it would come sooner than later. Maybe she would chastise him at breakfast. Daniel hoped she would not since he loved pancakes, and being scolded would ruin his breakfast.

Abby came down the stairwell before Daniel was finished setting the table and pouring milk. Papa held a cup of coffee in his hand as he rocked baby George. Mama was too busy to feed him at the moment, so Papa took his turn to keep the baby happy.

"Papa, I want to sit on your lap, too," Abby said while rubbing the sleep out of her eyes. As much as Abby loved her baby brother, she did not like giving up her position as the baby of the house. She resented not having all her daddy's attention since the birth of her new baby brother.

Papa set his coffee mug on the floor, shifted the baby to one arm, and held out his free hand to Abby. "I have a big lap, little darling.

Come on over and slide up here next to George. I can rock you both until breakfast is ready. Daniel is doing your chores right now, so you are free to rock with me."

Being totally unaware of what happened during the night, Abby said, "Thank you, Daniel."

Noticing William on the sofa for the first time, Abby exclaimed, "Is William sick? Why is he asleep on the sofa?"

Mama gave Papa a look from the kitchen. She was warning Papa not to tell Abby too much. She did not want the little girl to become upset and start crying.

"William took a little fall last night, and he broke his leg. He will be fine. He just has to rest his leg for several weeks, and then he will be back to normal," Papa said as he continued to rock his two children.

"Oh," said Abby, and then she added, "is he going to sleep on the sofa the whole time?"

Papa looked towards Mama. They did not have time to think through all the details of William's recuperation.

From the kitchen, Mama said, "William will stay on the sofa until he gets crutches. We will decide after we see how well he uses crutches whether he can go up and down the stairs safely. If he can, he will return to sleep in his own bed. Everyone, come to breakfast."

A platter was piled high with buckwheat pancakes, and Mama placed homemade jelly on the table as well as butter to spread on the hot pancakes. There were no silver maple or box elders on the farm, so if the family wanted syrup, they needed to buy it from the store. Mama said it was a luxury the family could not afford, but when she had extra sugar, she would make her own syrup from boiling water, sugar, and fruit flavoring. However, Mama said her jelly was better tasting.

No mention of the accident was brought up at breakfast, much to Daniel's relief. After eating, Daniel started to clear the table, but Papa reminded him that he had both his chores and William's chores to do, so he should leave the table and get started. Papa knew Daniel was tired from having no sleep and feeling stress, but the chores could not wait. The cows would become uncomfortable if they were not milked soon.

Daniel got to his feet and headed towards the door when William roused from his sleep. "Daniel, I am sorry I fell off the rafters and broke my leg. I know you have more work because of me."

Daniel stood in the doorway and said gently to his brother, "It was my fault you got hurt. It is only fair that I do your chores. You rest and get better. I will see you after the chores are done." Letting his eyes linger on his brother for only a moment, Daniel pushed the screen door open and went out to the barn.

Mama scurried to William's side to help him sit up. She said she would bring him a plate of pancakes if he felt like eating.

"Not right now, Mama. My stomach feels a bit queasy. Maybe in a little while, I will feel better. Right now, I think I just want to go back to sleep." William shut his eyes and went back into a deep sleep.

Mama looked at Papa with concern in her eyes. "Should William be feeling nauseated?"

Papa calmed Mama by saying, "It is probably just a side-effect from all the pain and the medication. I wouldn't worry about it. We will see how he feels when he wakes again."

Mama nodded in agreement and took the baby to feed him while the house was quiet and calm. Abby was drying the dishes Mama washed, and Papa went in to help put the dishes away. Many of the items were stored in high cupboards that Abby could not reach, even with a step ladder.

Papa left the house to help Daniel with the milking. There was no way Daniel could milk all the cows by himself. Even though Daniel had the best hands in the whole family for milking, it took a good fifteen minutes or more, depending on how cooperative each cow might be, to clean and milk her and get the milk poured into the larger container. With ten cows to milk, there was no way Daniel could milk them all without getting up at four in the morning. Usually, Daniel and William were up milking the cows by 5 AM, and together they could get all ten cows milked before breakfast and school during the week.

Daniel came in three hours later. The cows were milked, the animals fed, and the wood was chopped. The eggs would be gathered later by Abby or Mama. Papa usually took Sunday off from work unless there were repairs to be made on the equipment. Milk was in the springhouse, and it would need to be separated and cooled. Mama usually did that chore, but today, Daniel completed the task.

The pigeons caught from the night escapade were still in the crate, and Daniel knew he would need to do something about them, or they would die from lack of food, water, and heat. Stopping in the house for suggestions from Papa, Daniel asked, "Papa, I need to build a pigeon coop so the ones I caught don't die before I can get them to the store. I know we need every penny to pay for the hospital bill."

Papa got up from the chair. William was sleeping peacefully, and Mama was in the house if he needed something. "Hang on, Daniel, I have an idea of how we can build a coop for the birds you caught and keep the others from escaping when we want to catch them as well. I thought it might not be a bad idea to breed pigeons and doves. We could always use the extra money the birds would bring in. We would add it to the revenue the eggs, milk, cream, and vegetables bring in to the household."

Walking out into the yard, Papa told Daniel to go to the shed and bring the hammer and nails along with the wire cutter. Papa went to inspect the pile of lumber protected from the elements that Papa kept for repairs. Papa also looked at the large roll of chicken coop wire and calculated how much he would need for the project.

Before long, Papa was hammering nails into boards to build a deck upon the rafters. Daniel handed Papa board after board from the hayloft as he pushed further across the expanse. Once a sturdy floor was made, Papa walked to retrieve the wire. Leaving a small opening so the birds could fly into their regular perching spot, Papa enclosed the rest of the area with wire, including a top so the birds could not fly away from any direction. Papa built a door for Daniel to enter the loft.

"Once the birds have all come home to roost, we will close the opening, and they will be contained," Papa said. "You will need to put straw on the floor to collect the droppings which we can compost for fertilizer. You will also need to make sure they have clean water and feed to eat. Bring the crate and release the birds you caught last night. Soon the other pigeons and doves will return, settle down, and start to raise babies. If we do this right, we will have pigeons to sell as squab to the storekeeper, a good share of the year. It won't make us rich, but it could help when times are hard. I have a feeling this is going to be a year our crops won't do so well. I think it is going to be hot, dry and dusty."

Daniel thanked his father for all the work he put into building a coop for the pigeons and doves. Now, it would be easy to catch the birds when they wanted to take them to town to sell them. The hardest part would be trying to figure out which were the older birds and cull out the young tender ones for which the storekeeper would pay the highest price.

Papa suggested Daniel put away the tools and come into the house and take a nap. "You will have more chores again tonight and double in the morning, as well, until your brother is healed.

You are going to need to fight resentment towards your brother, you know."

"Papa, there is no way I am going to be resentful of William's injury. It was all my fault he got hurt. I should have been the one on the rafter. I just thought I might be too heavy, but now that I saw the rafters could hold your weight, I really feel bad."

Papa laughed. "Are you calling me fat?"

"No, Papa. I would never call you fat. At least, not to your face." Daniel joined his father in laughter. Daniel felt much better now the tension was released between his father and himself. Daniel knew Papa was not going to carry a grudge towards him for his stupidity.

Putting the tools away as directed, Daniel finally came into the house. It was mid-morning and too early for lunch. Daniel was feeling exhausted from the lack of sleep and all the chores.

"Go take a nap, son," Mama said as Daniel entered. "I will call you when it is time for lunch."

Daniel looked towards the sofa and saw William was still sleeping. He wondered how long it would take for the medication to wear off. He was fearful the pain would be intense once William no longer had any of it in his system.

Lying in his bed, Daniel thought about what he could do to make his brother feel better after the medication wore off. Daniel thought the weight of the blankets might be painful for William. Before falling asleep, Daniel came up with an idea of cutting out a large hole on opposite sides of a box. William's casted leg would need to fit through the holes so the box would take the weight of the comforter instead of resting on the leg. It seemed a good idea as Daniel drifted off to sleep.

William was awake when Daniel was called for lunch. Daniel stopped and talked to his brother before being seated at the table.

"Are you alright?" Daniel asked in all earnest.

Sighing, and adjusting his position on the sofa, William said, "That was awful. I have never been in so much pain in my whole life. I thought I would puke the whole way to the hospital. It was a good thing the doctor gave me an injection before they started to set my bone, or I would have died from the pain," William exaggerated.

"Do you remember how they set your bone or were you too groggy to know what they were doing?" William asked curiously.

"No, I remember. One does not forget getting strapped down and not being able to move while two huge men are either holding you in place or pulling on your leg. Even with the injection, it hurt like a son-of-a-gun. Luckily, the medicine made me sleepy, so I don't really remember the doctor putting on the strips of plaster of Paris to cast my leg. In fact, I don't remember the ride home. I just remember waking up on the sofa and Mama asking me if I wanted to eat pancakes," William said.

"What about now? Can you eat something if I make you a plate of food?" Daniel asked.

William answered, "Not anything too heavy. My stomach is still feeling a bit unsettled. I think I smell chicken soup. I bet Mama killed one of the old hens and made soup. I hope she made some noodles, too."

"You know noodles take a long time to dry. It is more likely Mama made dumplings to put in the soup. I like dumplings even better than noodles, so I will be happy," Daniel remarked.

Going into the kitchen to fetch William's lunch, Daniel was pleased to see he was right. Mama made a large pot of chicken and dumplings. Seeing Mama's smile, Daniel knew the lecture would not happen at this meal either.

CHAPTER FIVE

The first two weeks went by quickly for Daniel. He had no time for himself. Between chores, school, and more chores, the time flew by.

The time seemed endless for William. There was no way he could go to the outhouse. That meant having to relieve himself in a bucket by the side of the sofa. It was embarrassing and awkward. William hated to have his mother help him with the job of elimination. It had been a long time since he was a baby who needed his diapers changed, and now that is how he felt.

Most of the day was spent reading, doing homework that Daniel brought home, so William would not fall behind in his studies. That part of the day, William enjoyed. However, once he no longer had a new book to keep his attention, William became restless and irritable.

Abby played cards with William to entertain him. She also brought her dolly and tea set and expected William to play with her. On more than one occasion, Abby left in tears when William said some unkind words in his frustration.

"I am not a little girl, Abby. I don't want to play with your dumb doll or have a tea party. Now go away!" William would say harshly.

Mama would try to intervene, but she understood William was growing restless and hoped Papa would find a pair of crutches soon. Deloris said she gave the crutches away to another family a year ago, and she thought they donated the crutches to the second-hand store. She suggested Papa look in the store the next time he went to town.

Papa would be driving into town the following day. She would remind him and Daniel before they left with the eggs, pigeons, and butter to look in the second-hand store for the crutches. Papa was aware that William was becoming surly and needed to start getting around. Besides, Papa said William was losing muscle, and he needed the exercise.

The pigeons did not bring as much money as Daniel hoped. He gave the money to his father sadly, hoping to give more to help with the cost of the medical bills. The butter and eggs went towards the general fund Mama used to buy the things she needed. After the list was filled, Papa suggested that they drive over to the second-hand store to see if a pair of crutches might be available.

Relieved to find a pair of crutches, Papa used the money from the pigeons to pay for them. He explained to Daniel that the crutches were part of the medical bill. Daniel understood, but felt that meant he would need to contribute to the medical bill in other ways besides the pigeons. While Papa paid for the crutches, Daniel thought about hunting or trapping to help with the cost.

On the ride home, Daniel was given the reins, and Papa relaxed. "Papa, what do you think if I set some traps and I sell the furs to help with the hospital costs?"

Papa said it was a good idea, but Daniel must wait until winter for the furs to be worth anything. "Right now, the fur-bearing animals have thin coats because it is getting warm. In the winter, they will put on nice, thick coats, and the furs will be worth something. If we are still paying on the hospital bill in the winter, you can help by trapping or hunting."

Daniel let the subject drop. Winter was a long way away, and there would be plenty to do with planting in the spring and later, harvesting the crops. In the fall, hogs would need to be butchered, and fat rendered into lard. Papa would smoke hams and bacon, and Mama would make sausages that would be stored in crocks covered with the rendered lard and stored in the cool cellar along with vegetables and fruit from the garden and orchard. There would be plenty of work until winter to keep both boys busy once William was back on his feet.

Daniel was thinking about how nice it would be to have William back by his side. He missed his brother's company as well as his help with the chores.

It seemed only days after getting the crutches that William could use them as long as he did not put any weight on his broken leg. Finally, William was able to leave the house and go outside for fresh air. At first, William was slow on the crutches. In the evenings, William complained of pain in his arms and back from using muscles he rarely used before breaking his leg. Mama gave William back rubs, and William purred like a kitten.

Days passed, and William was proving to everyone how fast he could walk on crutches. Challenging Abby to a race, William almost beat her to the line Daniel drew in the dirt. When Mama looked out the door and watched the race, she didn't know if she should stop it since falling could cause William a setback or be overjoyed at the progress William was making towards a full recovery. Walking out with George balanced on her hip, Mama quietly told William and Abby to stop racing so William did not get hurt and went back into the house knowing her children would come up with another game equally as dangerous.

'What can a mother do?' thought Mama to herself as she gave a backward glance at her children and noticed them plotting just as she knew they would. The baby needed changing, and there was a basket load of dirty diapers to wash. There was no time to police her older children.

Tomorrow William was going back to school. He was excited to return to studying. He kept up with his schoolwork at home, but it was not the same as being in school and showing off how smart he was to his teacher and the other students. William knew some of the boys disliked him, but he had not put two and two together yet, which was odd for such a smart boy. Some of the older boys didn't like the fact that William, who was younger, was better at reading, writing, and arithmetic, as well as history and geography. It made them feel stupid, and those boys didn't like feeling stupid.

Daniel was excited that Papa let him drive the wagon to school so that William could ride. Daniel hopped off the wagon, went around to the passenger side, and held William's crutches as William struggled to get down using only one leg. Once William was set and balanced, Daniel handed him his crutches and got back onto the seat of the wagon to drive the team where they could be comfortable for the school day.

William, showing off his new skills with his crutches, swung his good leg to make the next step while balancing on the crutches. Setting his crutches, swinging through, and taking the next step proved to be almost a game. Smiling at the crowd gathered to watch his progress, William was feeling like the king of the playground until Henry stuck out his foot, catching one of the crutches, sending William falling face-first into the dirt.

Before anyone could see if William was hurt, Henry was lying on the ground beside William. Standing over, Henry was Daniel, red-faced and angry.

"If you ever hurt my little brother again, I will do more than punch you in the face!" Daniel seethed as he made the threat. Daniel continued to stand over Henry with his hands formed into fists.

Scurrying quickly to his feet and backing off, Henry knew Daniel meant every word he said. Rushing to the safety of a group of older boys, Henry heard one boy say, "You mess with one of the Dolen boys, and you have both to fight."

Even most of the older boys gave Daniel a wide berth. Almost six feet tall and not even in his teens yet, Daniel was big for his age. Working hard on the farm, Daniel had large muscles that even the older boys envied. William, being slight of build, felt protected by his older brother, and that gave him a cockiness that occasionally got him in trouble. This was one of those days.

Daniel helped his brother to his feet and retrieved the pair of crutches. Glowering at Henry, Daniel dared him to try that maneuver again. Slipping back behind the other boys, Henry hid and made a face.

Miss Turnbull, unaware of what happened, stepped out of the schoolhouse to ring the bell. Little Eloise was about to tell on Henry when Becky pulled her aside and told her not to tell.

"If you tell on Henry, Daniel will get in trouble for hitting him in the face. It is best to just be quiet. Everything is settled, and William is not hurt. Okay?" Becky asked.

Eloise nodded and glanced at William. Even though he was several years older than she was, Eloise thought he was the cutest and smartest boy in the county. Becky kept her eyes on Daniel.

CHAPTER SIX

Mama declared she would not be going to the barn dance with baby George, and neither would William be allowed to go. She said that the climb up to the hayloft where the dance floor was erected would not be easy to climb with a baby in arms, and indeed, William would struggle with the cast still on his leg. Objecting loudly, William complained about how unfair his mother's decision was, but Papa gave one warning look, and William stopped complaining.

That meant Daniel and Abby would need to take a bath after chores. Good school clothes would be worn, and Mama fussed with Abby's hair ribbons. With everyone scrubbed and clean, Papa grabbed his fiddle, and Daniel was allowed to drive the team and wagon. Papa wanted to warm up his fiddle on the drive.

The three merrily traveled down the road to Juergen's barn, where the barn dance would be held. Papa played familiar songs, and everyone joined in singing until they turned into the yard and found a spot to leave the wagon and team. Daniel was charged with the task of making sure the wagon brake was on, and the horses were hobbled, secured and left with oat treats in their feedbags, before joining the family in the large barn.

The red barn was built before the family's house, and it was prized. More money was spent on the barn than on the house where the family lived. The barn was huge with a high-pitched roof. Stalls for the animals were on the ground level. The cows and horses were turned out in the adjoining pen for the evening. The hayloft was swept clean. Space was made available for the dance party since the hay was not yet been harvested and stored. A table was placed at the far end for the assortment of cookies, cakes, and pies and punch the women provided. Children were allowed to be on the dance floor if they were old enough to be safe. The little ones played behind the seating area. Parents kept them away from the railings and the risk of falling to the floor below.

Many families were already gathered when Papa arrived with his fiddle. Daniel, hurriedly came into the barn to see if any of his friends arrived before him. Several girls giggled in the seating area, and Daniel glance to see if they were looking at him. He noted one girl, Becky, from school was smiling at him. Later, Daniel thought he might get up the courage to ask her to dance.

The fiddlers made themselves comfortable at the far end of the loft. Papa would call out square dance moves as he fiddled with two of his friends. They were playing together for several years, and each knew the songs that would be played. Mainly country style dances dominated. However, Polka was also popular, and one of the musicians took out an accordion to play the upbeat tunes.

The ladies were all wearing their Sunday best dresses, and the men wore their Sunday-go-to-meeting clothes as well. Smiles were on everyone's faces in anticipation of the fun and fellowship the evening would present.

Seeing Abby playing with a school friend, Daniel walked towards her, stopping to chat with schoolmates along the way. Soon the dancing would begin, and the boys would gather at the food table. Mrs. Granger's cookies and cakes were already placed on the table, along with many other tempting treats. With the parents busy dancing and socializing, the boys knew they would be able to eat more than they should and get away with it.

As the fiddlers begin to play tunes, Daniel watched in amusement as Oscar got up the nerve to ask Miss Turnbull to dance. Accepting with pleasure dancing., the two went into the center of the barn and faced each other. Couples crowded the floor and squared-off into groups of eight for the first square dance. Everyone knew the moves as Papa fiddled and called, "Circle left, Do Sa Do, swing your partner, Promenade right, Weave the ring, Allemande left, Ladies Star right, and on and on."

With little ringlets of perspiration forming on the strands of hair that came untucked from Miss Turnbull's neat bun, she laughed and thanked her dance partner as she turned to go back and sit with the other ladies. Oscar, not wanting his time to end with the pretty young teacher, offered to fetch her a cup of punch. Smiling, Miss Turnbull accepted Oscar's kind offer.

The boys were at the table, munching on cookies when Oscar arrived. Ignoring his classmates, he pushed through them to pour a cup of punch.

"Oscar has a girlfriend...a girlfriend...a girlfriend!" started one of the boys in a sing-song voice.

"Knock it off! You know, Miss Turnbull is not my girlfriend. I just wanted to make sure she got to dance. She doesn't know many people in our community," Oscar said in his defense.

All eyes turned to Miss Turnbull, who was accepting an offer to dance from a good-looking young man that everyone recognized as the new pastor in town.

"Looks like you might as well drink that cup of punch. Miss Turnbull is going to be too busy to drink it for quite some time," chuckled Daniel while Oscar's lips formed a frown.

Oscar belted the cup of punch down and walked away to the laughter of his schoolmates. Daniel left the group to return to talk with Abby. His mother had given him strict orders to watch his little sister and make sure she stayed safe.

"Please, please," pleaded Abby as she tugged on her brother's arm, trying hard to pull him to his feet. "Dance with me."

Daniel finally got to his feet. He took his little sister's hand and led her to the dance floor. Before long, Daniel was having fun as he twirled Abby around the floor. Abby giggled and giggled and pleaded for Daniel to swing her around more. Papa came to Daniel's rescue and cut in. Daniel left the dance floor while Abby stood on her father's feet as he danced her around the floor.

Before the next dance was started, grandfathers and granddaughters, uncles and nieces, as well as brothers and sisters, were all dancing gleefully. No one teased Daniel about dancing with his little sister. Before long, grandsons were merrily promenading their grandmothers around the barn floor as Daniel turned to Mrs. Granger to see if she would like to dance. The barn dance was intergenerational entertainment, and no one was left sitting for long.

The musicians and their families were the last to leave the barn dance. Everyone was exhausted but happy. The social event was a success, and besides an occasional upset stomach from one child or another eating too many cookies and cakes, everyone said it was the best time they had had for a very long time. Plans were made for another barn dance for the following month.

Abby was curled up in the wagon with her head on Daniel's lap, while she slept peacefully all the way home. Upon arrival, Papa carried Abby to her bed, and mother helped to change her into her nightgown.

"I hope my cast is off by next month," William said in a pout. "It wasn't much fun for Mama and me to be home with the baby while you stuffed your face with cookies and pie. You didn't think to bring me home a treat, did you?"

"Don't worry, Dear," Mother remarked as she returned downstairs, "you will have your cast off, and you will be back to normal. In fact, I think you will return to the doctor's office next week. He will decide then if you can remove the cast or if you need to leave it on for another week or two. At any rate, I am sure it will be off by the next barn dance."

Whispering, Daniel said, "And you will be able to milk your share of the cows again."

Giving Daniel a dirty look at the last remark, made Daniel laugh as he held out two broken cookies in his clean white kerchief, he managed to bring home for his brother. A smile passed quickly over William's face when he saw the treats. It seemed William would forgive Daniel if bribed.

CHAPTER SEVEN

The day came when William finally got his cast removed. The doctor told him he was good as new. William knew that was not entirely true. His leg looked skinny compared to his other leg, but the doctor told him with exercise, his mended leg would build muscle quickly.

Getting back to his daily chores was not pleasant. William enjoyed being the center of his mother's attention when Abby or baby George was not demanding her care. When the two smaller children were napping, and Mother's chores were done, William would enjoy listening to stories read from the Bible. He particularly liked the one where a small shepherd boy triumphed over a giant. Now, those days were gone, and William was back to milking and feeding the cows and the other animals. In the evenings, homework took most of his time.

Spring planting was next. Before William's medical bills were compiled, the family purchased a new John Deere plow that the company claimed that dirt would not stick to it. This improvement meant the horses could plow faster, and oxen were no longer needed. Now, one member could drive the team while sitting on the seat of the plow. That freed up the family members who used to need to walk behind to steer the old plow while another needed to clean off or scour the blade frequently. With the new plow, it was still hard, hot work, but so much better than before. Father did most of the plowing while William stayed at home to help with the other chores. Daniel still took his usual position next to the plow.

After sweating all day long out in the field, Mama would insist that Daniel wash up before coming in to eat. She would quietly say, "Daniel, you are growing up, and you are starting to sweat like a grown man. That means you will need to wash more frequently, or no one will want to be around you. Go wash up with soap and water now."

Papa was already washing up. It was just part of his regular routine. "Don't want to offend the ladies, Daniel. Someday you will understand what I mean by that," Papa said with a chuckle.

"If you mean that I will want to kiss a girl, you are wrong! Girls are creepy." Daniel said with a wrinkled-up nose.

William, who was sent to hurry Papa and Daniel to dinner, heard Daniel's comment. "I know two girls you would kiss today. I see you looking at Becky at school and Ellie every time we go into the store. Daniel likes gir-ulls, Daniel likes gir-ulls," William sang as he dodged the washcloth Daniel hurled at him.

Papa laughed and put his arm around Daniel's shoulder. "Girls aren't so bad. I think you are starting to realize that already. Remember, your mama used to be a girl."

Walking to his chair at the table, Daniel continued to glower at his little brother. Mama saw the look and asked what was wrong.

"Just growing pains, my dear," Papa said and smiled.

Mama knew to let the subject drop at dinner. She would find out what happened once the children were all in bed.

"William, I need you to bring over the pot on the stove, but be careful. Little George needs to be changed. The rest of you go ahead and eat. I won't be long," Mama said as she carted George away to her bedroom to change the baby's diaper.

"Pee you! George stinks. I am glad Mama took him away. I almost lost my appetite," Abby said disgustedly.

"Where did such a little girl learn such a big word as appetite?" Papa asked Abby teasingly.

"I know lots of big words. I know elephant, giraffe, hippomotymus..." Abby stated but was interrupted by William.

"You mean hippopotamus. It isn't hippomotymus," William corrected.

"It is so...it is hippomotymus, isn't it Papa?" Abby said while standing and stomping her foot.

"I have never been to Africa. Why are you asking me?" Papa said, trying hard not to be drawn into the argument.

"Children, stop!" Mama said as she returned, carrying a better smelling baby boy.

"But Mama..." both children said at once.

"I said, stop, and I mean it. Our dinner will not be ruined by petty arguments. Now, pass the potatoes and sit back down, young lady. We do not stomp our feet whenever we are mad. That is not acceptable in this house," Mama said sternly.

Sitting back down, William whispered, "Hippopotamus."

"Mama," howled Abby, now in tears, "William said hippopotamus to me."

"William, leave the table. You can skip dinner tonight if you can't behave. I told you to stop tormenting your sister. Go to your room!" Mama growled.

Pushing his chair aside, William stomped out of the room but not without saying his mind, "You want Abby to be stupid the rest of her life?"

"Mama," wailed Abby even louder, "I am not stupid!"

Papa knew he needed to intervene at this point. Dinner was ruined. Getting up from his chair, he followed William to his room. Abby continued to cry, which caused baby George to cry, and Mama left the table to go to the rocking chair to soothe the baby. Daniel continued to eat, helping himself to another portion of meat and potatoes.

"No sense letting Williams dinner go to waste. I may as well eat it or the hogs will," William said aloud to himself.

The next day things were back to normal except Papa had a fever. "You are taking the day off, Harlan," Mama said after touching Papa's forehead. "You are burning up. The boys can do the chores. I don't think to miss a day of school will hurt either one of them. Well, maybe Daniel, but he can make up the homework."

"I don't know. I have several more acres that need to be plowed to stay on schedule," Papa said, trying to get to his feet.

Pushing Papa back down on the bed, Mama said, "You aren't doing anything today and maybe not even tomorrow."

Getting the boys up, Mama told them that Papa was sick, and they would need to stay home from school today to do the chores Papa would have been doing.

"I can finish the plowing," Daniel said. "With the new plow, it is super-duper easy."

"I will run that past your father. You and William take care of the milk cows and come back in for breakfast. I will have pancakes and eggs ready by the time you finish your morning chores," Mama said as the boys got out of bed and reached for their work clothes.

Not quite light outside, William and Daniel raced to the barn. The aroma of warm straw and hot cows mixed in the air as they opened the barn door wide enough to step inside. The manure would need to be shoveled out of the milking stalls after feeding the cows. Then the cows needed a thorough cleaning before milking. Each boy was milking for years, and they did everything automatically.

"I hear they have invented the milking machine," William said over his shoulder to his older brother.

"You have to be kidding," Daniel remarked. "That would be great not to need to milk ever again. I bet the machine is expensive. I doubt we will be able to afford one for a very long time, at least, not until we get the medical bills paid."

The boys stopped talking and concentrated on getting the morning chores done so they could eat. Working quickly, it was not long before they heard Mama ringing the bell to let them know breakfast was ready.

Racing once more, Daniel, with his long legs, reached the porch first. "Hold on, boys. You both need to wash up. I will help this morning with separating the cream from the milk so Daniel can start plowing," Mama said as she blocked the screen door.

The family ate quietly so that Papa could get more rest. Mama made oatmeal for Papa to eat while the rest of the family ate bacon and eggs with pancakes.

William went about his chores while Mama cleaned the breakfast dishes, reminding him she would be out soon to help him with separating the milk. Daniel rushed to the barn to get the team hitched to the plow. Papa allowed him to plow on several occasions, so he felt he knew what to do.

The morning was turning warm, and Daniel knew it was going to be rather hot by the time he finished with the plowing. Figuring it made sense to get as much done as quickly as possible caused Daniel to rush. Not looking ahead as well as he should, Daniel found himself surrounded by angry bumblebees. He did not see the nest in the underground borough and plowed right through it.

The bees massed and zoned in on the intruders. Buzzing angrily and stinging the team, the horses panicked, eyes wide in fear, ears pinned back. The team started to run, tails flagging high, dumping Daniel to the ground and pulling the plow wobbling side to side behind them. Fortunately, the bees concentrated on the larger animals and seemed to miss Daniel totally as he laid in the tall grass that was waiting to be plowed. Knowing the damage, the horses would do to the new plow as they dragged it towards home, Daniel got to his feet and raced after them.

He found the horses grazing some distance from where they were first attacked by the bees. It was far enough away that the bees gave up their pursuit and returned to their nest. The plow laid on its side but seemed oddly undamaged.

Daniel righted the plow and inspected all the parts. The clevis or hitch was still attached to the team, the brace was slightly bent but not so severely that Papa could not straighten it. The moldboard, with its cutting edge or share, seemed only dulled, but not chipped or broken. The point could be sharpened to allow it to break through the clods of dirt. Daniel felt as though he was very fortunate until he saw the welts on the horses' rumps.

The horses each had several bee stingers left in their rumps from the angry bees before being able to outrun them. Daniel unhitched the team from the plow and led them home. He knew he needed to remove the stingers and treat the wounds, hoping neither horse would have an allergic reaction to the bee venom. Daniel heard how one neighbor lost a horse when it was stung multiple times by bees. Daniel knew that losing one of the team would devastate the planting season.

Once back at the barn, Daniel found a dull knife and removed each stinger, still clinging to the horses. Being careful not to allow the venom sac to be pressed, which would have caused more venom to pour into the wound, Daniel proceeded. After the stingers were removed, Daniel went to the house to ask his mama for vinegar and baking soda. He knew it would help to neutralize the poison and reduce the pain each horse must be feeling.

"Daniel, why do you need vinegar and baking soda?" Mama asked as Daniel rummaged through the pantry.

"Maud and Molly got stung by bees. I got the stingers out, but I need to do something for the welts. You always used vinegar and baking soda on us when we got stung. I figured it would work for the horses as well," Daniel answered.

Papa woke when he heard the conversation. Staggering out of the bedroom, Papa asked what happened.

"We hit a bumblebee's nest," Daniel answered honestly. "I didn't see it. Everything is alright. The plow seems like it is only going to need to have the share sharpened, and the horses ran fast enough that they only got a few stings. Once I give the horses first aid, I will take them back out and bring the plow back home."

"Let me get dressed. I will go with you," Papa said wearily.

"Oh no, you don't. You will stay in bed until I say you can get up!" Mama barked. "The baby is asleep, Abby and William are both here, so they can take care of him if he wakes while I am gone. I will go with Daniel to check the horses, and if I feel they should rest, we will get the plow tomorrow. I doubt you will be very far behind."

"I got most of the plowing done in the north section before I hit the bumblebees' nest. I think we are about on schedule. I can get old Saul hitched to bring back the plow if Mama says the team has to rest. I can sharpen the point yet today. I still have daylight left to do the work. I might need your help to straighten the brace, but it isn't all that bad. I probably could pound out the bend myself...." Daniel let the sentence hang, hoping his father would not become angry.

"Go back to bed Papa, you still have a fever," Mama said. "I will go see if there is more damage than what Daniel thinks. If he can't fix things himself, I will ask William to ride over to get Oscar to help. He is eighteen and surely knows how to fix a bent brace. The children are all out of school by now," Mama offered.

Papa relented and went back into the bedroom to lie down. Abby came into the house to watch George in case he woke up. William was told to continue gathering eggs, and doing his other chores, but to stay close in case Abby needed his help. Grabbing the vinegar and baking soda, Daniel and Mama went back out to the barn.

The horses were munching on hay and did not seem to be in any distress. Both were breathing fine, so Mama was sure neither was having an allergic reaction to the bee venom. Making a paste out of the vinegar and baking soda, which fizzled as they two reacted to each other, Daniel and Mama went about patting it onto each wound, as the horses sniffed the air at the odd smell.

Mama announced the team would be fine to go and bring back the plow. She said she would return to inspect the plow once Daniel returned, but not wanting to leave the baby or Papa for long, Mama walked back to the house.

Walking the team back to the north section, Daniel hitched the plow and walked behind, guiding the team home without adding his weight to the plow. Once home, Mama announced the damage was very little, and Daniel could ask William to give him a hand with the repairs. Mama's voice rang in Daniel's mind as he let the words relax the knots in his shoulder. "No real damage was done. I am glad you weren't stung by those nasty bees."

CHAPTER EIGHT

Spring gave way to early summer. The school year was almost over, and planting was completed. Corn and wheat were growing, and the days were becoming hotter. Daniel and William were studying hard to make sure they passed all the tests that Miss Turnbull would be giving them. William was feeling confident, but Daniel was not feeling quite as good about the up-and-coming tests.

In the evening, Mama sat down with Daniel at the table. Tutoring him on any subject except arithmetic, Mama beamed with Daniel's progress. "You are going to do just fine. Now, if we can just get your papa to sit down and help you with your numbers, you might do even better than William."

William didn't like hearing Mama praising Daniel. William had always been the scholar in the family, and there was no way Daniel would outshine him on any of the tests. With renewed vigor, William stayed up later and later each night studying.

The day of the tests came, and Mama had trouble getting William up and out of bed to do his chores before going to school. Mama sternly said, "William, you get up right this minute. Why are you so tired? How long did you stay up studying last night?"

"Mama, I am too tired to do my chores. Can't I skip them this morning and get a little more sleep before going to school?" William said while turning over and pulling his blanket over his head.

"No! You get up right this minute, or I will send your father in to get you up," Mama scolded.

Dragging himself out of bed and pulling on his work clothes to go out to do chores, William resentfully walked out to the barn to milk his share of the cows. Daniel was already on his milking stool with a bucket almost full of warm milk.

"What took you so long, lazybones?" Daniel said in the way of greeting with a huge smile crossing his face. "I have already milked two cows, and I am almost finished with my third."

"Yeah, yeah, yeah," grumbled William. "Well, I will catch up with you in no time. I can milk twice as many cows as you at the same time. Don't think so, then do the math."

Daniel laughed as he saw William yawn and start to close his eyes. "Better not fall asleep on that ole cow's hip. She is bound to kick you if you do."

Daniel took pity on his brother and milked two of his cows while William struggled to stay awake. Putting all the milk into the spring house for Mama to separate, the boys went into breakfast. Once changed into clean clothes, the boys rode Jack to school, not forgetting his hobbles.

Miss Turnbull greeted the children at the door with a smile. She would be returning to her hometown to continue her own studies during the summer. She was looking forward to the summer break as much as the children. Oscar gave Miss Turnbull his present as he entered the schoolhouse.

Oscar was the only student who was older than the eighth grade. Oscar's father died when he was only five, and his mother needed him to stay close to home. Oscar was not able to attend the high school in the nearest town, so arrangements were made for Oscar to remain at the one-room schoolhouse with Miss Turnbull to continue his education. Oscar missed school frequently since he was the man of the house but attended school as often as he could.

"Oscar, these ribbons are beautiful. I will wear them in my hair. This is your last year in my class. What will you be doing with your future?"

As the children were seated, Miss Turnbull addressed them all. "Your first test will be a written test. I want each of you to write what you plan to do once you finish school. Remember, I will be checking your grammar, punctuation, penmanship, and spelling. This is a test, so you cannot use the dictionary or any of your books. You have one hour to write and rewrite if necessary. The time starts now."

Paper was passed out, and the children busily started writing. Miss Turnbull knew the younger children's stories would be fantasy, and she looked forward to reading each paper. From past experience, Miss Turnbull knew little Eloise would write about becoming a princess, even though she would misspell the word. The older children would write more realistically, but with equal amounts of dreams for the future.

Time was called, and Miss Turnbull gathered the papers. "You will have one more test before I give you a recess break. I want to see how well each of you is doing in arithmetic. You will notice if you are not keeping your eyes on your own paper, that each of you has a different test depending on your age. Once again, you will have one hour to complete the test. If you finish before the hour, I want you to double-check your answers. If you are sure the answers are correct, then quietly bring the test to my desk, and you may start your recess early. I don't want anyone to rush through the test so they can have more time to play. Do your best. Now you may start."

William flew through the test. There were exactly one hundred different problems for him to calculate. Some students needed more than a minute to solve each problem, but William could do each problem in less than thirty seconds. Finishing in less than the time allotted, William double-checked his work, and sure it was correct, he took the test paper to Miss Turnbull's desk.

Smiling, Miss Turnbull nodded to the door, and William quietly left the building to enjoy the early summer day. As children filed out of the school, one at a time, no one noticed that William was not playing outside. Games were started as more of the children came out into the sunshine. Twenty minutes after the last test was gathered, Miss Turnbull called the children back into the classroom to start their next test.

Passing out maps of the United States, each child, depending on their grade level, had multiple questions to answer. Miss Turnbull was about to tell the class that the time was about to begin when she noticed William missing from his seat.

"Daniel, where is your brother?" Miss Turnbull inquired. "He should have come in with the rest of the class."

"I don't know, Mam. I was playing with Henry, and I didn't even notice William was not around. He often takes a book and reads under the tree. Shall I go out and find him?" Daniel asked.

"No, you need to start your test. Oscar, you are exempt from this test anyway. Would you mind finding William?" Miss Turnbull questioned.

Oscar jumped out of his seat. He would do anything for Miss Turnbull. As he went out of the door, the rest of the students were directed to their test papers. The test time was started.

When Oscar did not come straight back with William, Daniel became worried. His eyes kept fleeting towards the back of the classroom to the door.

"Daniel, you need to keep your eyes on your test paper. I don't want to think that you are cheating," Miss Turnbull warned.

Daniel's eyes returned to his paper, but his ears strained to hear the door opening. When it finally did open with some effort, all eyes turned to the back. Oscar entered carrying a sleeping William.

"I found him in your buggy fast asleep. I couldn't wake him, so I just carried him," Oscar said as he waited for Miss Turnbull to tell him where to put the sleeping boy.

"Daniel, how late has your brother been staying up to study?" Miss Turnbull asked as she directed Oscar to bring William to his seat.

"Wake up!" Miss Turnbull said as she shook William.

Opening his eyes, William visibly alarmed at seeing he was in Oscar's arms, found he was now the brunt of the jokes as the children laughed and called him a big baby.

"That is enough, class!" Miss Turnbull reprimanded. "Set William down, Oscar." More quietly, Miss Turnbull continued, "William, you still have time to complete this test. Please start now and class, I want everyone to quiet down and stop sniggering."

Giving William a pat of sympathy on his shoulder, Miss Turnbull returned to her desk to correct the last two tests given. Even with the warning, William could hear the occasional giggle and knew he was the brunt of the joke. Face reddening from humiliation, William tried hard to focus all his attention on completing the test.

Lunch was called, and the children grabbed their lunchboxes. The students were directed outdoors to eat since it was a beautiful day, and Miss Turnbull was using her lunchtime to continue correcting tests. With hopes of leaving by the weekend for her home, Miss Turnbull wanted no distractions during this time.

Filing out of doors with lunch boxes, the students gathered into small groups to eat on the steps of the building, under trees, or at the one picnic table reserved for the older girls who did not want their dresses to become soiled.

William and Daniel ate together under the tree far from the giggles that continued to plague William. William was moody and irritable at becoming the brunt of the joke.

"Why didn't you come and find me? That was so embarrassing to have Oscar carry me into class like a baby. I will never live this down!" William fumed.

"Oh, come on. It was not that bad. The kids will all forget by next fall when we return. Think of it this way; you won't see hardly any of our classmates until fall, except at church, and not all of our classmates go to our church," Daniel said, trying to comfort his little brother.

"I suppose you are right, but I still have to get through today, and here comes Henry and his gang now," William said with dread.

As the small group of boys came over, laughing and pointing at William, one of the boys put his thumb in his mouth and pretended to be a baby. Seeing this, Daniel got to his feet.

"I won't have a bit of trouble beating all three of you if you don't stop teasing William right this moment! I might just shove your thumb down your throat, Richard, if you keep it up," Daniel said intimidatingly.

All three boys found the grins leaving their faces as they looked into the eyes of Daniel and knew he meant what he just said. Henry took the lead and turned to leave but not without having to get one final jab in.

"It seems the big baby can't handle our teasing. He needs his big brother to protect him," sneered Henry under his breath to his fellow conspirators.

"Watch it!" Daniel said without a bit of humor. "William won't always be as small as he is now, and he has a good memory, as do I."

All three boys turned and returned to their section of the playground. Henry hit Richard and said, "Tag, you are it," and the game was on, and the teasing stopped.

Daniel found he would have liked to have been part of the game, but he was not about to leave his brother's side while he was vulnerable. Daniel found himself wondering whether William would ever get taller. A part of Daniel didn't like having to protect him all the time.

The afternoon continued with the last few tests. Miss Turnbull walked to the windows often as she became aware that the usual afternoon breeze was missing. The air, too still, was becoming moist and warm, and the skies were taking on an ominous yellow cast.

"Class, I think everyone should leave now. If you aren't finished with your test, I will collect it anyway. I want everyone to quickly gather your belongings and head home directly," Miss Turnbull directed, trying not to sound alarmed.

Living in Tornado Alley meant that storms were imminent at this time of the year, and people made plans for such events. All the children knew they needed to get home and help the family prepare in case a tornado should form with the approaching thunderstorm.

Soon, the classroom was bare of lunch pails, book bags, or other belongings of the students, and the children were running home or riding their horses at top speeds. Miss Turnbull watched them leave with apprehension for their safety, filling her thoughts.

William, behind Daniel, was holding on as tight as possible as Jack ran towards their farm. Papa was already outside, opening the barn doors to allow Maud, Molly, and old Saul to be turned loose in the pasture in case a tornado formed. It was always a hard decision as to whether the horses would be safer in the barn from the hail or whether they should be loose to outrun a tornado. The horses instinctively knew where they would find protection from the hail, and they bolted away and out of sight in seconds.

Jumping off Jack, Daniel led the pony to the gate, removed his tack, and let him run free to follow the other horses. The cows were already out to pasture to graze. They, too, seemed to know where to go to be safe. Daniel watched Jack momentarily until his father shouted for him to make sure his mother, the baby, and Abby were heading down to the storm cellar.

Looking to the sky, Daniel saw the dark greenish sky with a wall cloud forming. He knew the approaching clouds would be filled with debris and hail would soon be pelting the ground.

Father looked towards his crops and hoped the hail would not damage the new sprouts. The crops were needed to finance his farm and keep his family and livestock fed for the next year. The weather was always an unknown factor in whether or not the family would survive another year on the farm.

Knowing the chickens would most likely go into the chicken house once the sky became darkened, William abandoned his attempts to shoo them inside. If they did not go inside, he knew they would roost in trees or head for some other shelter. The chickens were the last of his concerns at the moment.

Grabbing Shep, the beloved family dog, William raced for the storm cellar on his father's command. Over the top of the hill, William saw a violently rotating column of air, dropping from the cloud, hovering menacingly in the sky barely above the ground. If it descended to the earth, a tornado would form, which would destroy most anything in its path.

William stood transfixed as he watched the whirling energetic glow in the clouds from the lightning strikes smacking the puddled ground. The rotating mass lowered from the darkening sky filling instantly with dust and debris as it touched the ground… 'Oh, My! A TORNADO JUST TOUCHED DOWN…NEAR ME'!

Which way it would travel now was unpredictable. It could stay on the ground for twenty minutes traveling from 30 to 70 miles per hour, or it could bounce around the hills, hitting or missing farms until it dissipated. In the meantime, the hail was pelting everything around him.

Waking from his trance, William rushed to the storm cellar. Mama, Abby, and baby George were already inside. Daniel returned to Papa to see what else might need to be done before they, too, could take shelter.

Mama called for Shep, who warily looked inside the dark storm shelter. Shep, slept on the porch all year except during blizzards when he was allowed into the house.

"Come on, Shep. You can make it down the stairs," Mama encouraged as William pushed the big dog from behind.

Shep, unaccustomed to stairs, was hesitant, but with encouragement, he managed to gingerly step down each step until he was at the bottom. William raced down the stairs behind the dog as Papa and Daniel stormed in, closing the large double doors behind them.

"Whew! That was close. I sure am glad your teacher let you out of class early. I would have hated for you two boys to be out in this storm," Papa said earnestly.

Lamps were lit by Mama when she entered the storm cellar with Abby and the baby. Abby insisted that Mama light as many lamps as was stored in the cellar. Abby was not sure they would not be greeted by snakes. She remembered her older brothers teasing how snakes would live in the cellar.

Looking around, Papa took a mental inventory of everything he stored in the cellar for a time such as now. He had food and medicine for any injured animal that might be harmed during the storm. Storing enough food for all the livestock took a lot of room in the cellar, but if the barn were destroyed by the tornado, the food would be necessary to keep his livestock alive while rebuilding. Medicine for injured or sick animals had been advised by the county agent. That, too, was stored in the cellar.

With a pond on the farm property and a well, Papa stored very little water. He had enough for the family if they needed to stay put for hours, but that was about all he stored. If the windmill were destroyed, Papa would need to rebuild quickly, but not so soon as those farmers who were not as fortunate to have a pond on their land.

Papa counted his blessings, starting with the fact that his family was safe. After the storm, he and the boys would need to go and search for the livestock and bring them home to evaluate injuries any animal might have sustained from the hail, flying debris, or their own panicked actions. Broken bones were not uncommon when animals fled from storms.

Papa thought of how much the family would lose if the house were destroyed. All their furnishings, clothes, and the few valued photographs would be lost. He strained to hear if the horrifying sounds of a tornado were above them. Papa knew people said the wind sounded like a freight train and was glad he did not hear that noise.

Even if the tornado moved into another direction, or bounced over the farm completely, the wind shear alone could cause incredible damage. With winds blowing from 100 to 300 miles per hour, anything not well built would be swept away. Papa knew the house and barn would remain standing, but that did not mean that shingles on the roof would not need repairing, and damage to the contents of the buildings from the hail would not be a factor.

The younger children huddled next to their mama while baby George slept unaware of the storm. Mama was glad for that blessing. It would be hard to calm the children with the baby crying loudly. With him asleep, Mama told stories to her brood that helped to take their minds off the storm.

When no further sounds could be heard from the surface, Papa said he was going to go outside to make sure it was clear. Opening one of the cellar doors at the top of the stairs, Papa pushed the other heavy door aside to allow himself to climb out onto the ground.

Looking around and surveying the damage, Papa saw many limbs broken from trees lying on the ground around the property. Removing them, sawing or axing them into firewood would be the easiest part of the cleanup.

Chickens were once more pecking the ground and acting undisturbed by the storm that passed. Papa knew he may have lost a chicken or two but was less concerned about their loss as the egg loss that may follow due to the chickens being stressed by the storm. He knew chickens stopped laying when upset.

"Boys, come on out. We have some work to do," Papa shouted down the cellar stairs.

William, Daniel, followed by Shep, came up the stairs. Daniel surveyed the damage, as well.

"I think we were lucky, Papa. It doesn't look like too much bad happened. The roof on the barn looks okay. We might need to go up and nail down a few shingles, but otherwise, I don't see any large holes," Daniel said, acting like a grown man.

Papa looked at his oldest son with love, causing his chest to swell with pride, almost bursting the buttons off his shirt. He knew he could count on Daniel to do his job without complaint. William, too, knew when to step up and try to do a man's work.

"You want us to go and round up the livestock?" Daniel asked.

Papa answered, "Yes, that would be a big help. I will get your mother, Abby, and the baby settled back into the house, and then I will join you. I am proud of you, boys. You did a good job of doing exactly what we planned if a tornado hit. We were lucky this time...."

Shep barked excitedly as he ran circles around the boys who were heading out to the pastures in search of the horses and cows. Shep knew he was going to get to do what he did best—round up the cows. He could hardly wait to be nipping at their heels and heading them back to the barn.

Once out in the pasture, Daniel signaled Shep with a whistle and a hand signal. The big farm dog loped off to find the cows, barking with his joy. Seeing a small herd down in the ravine, Shep ran wide to head them toward the boys.

"William, you stay with Shep and this group of cows and get them back to the barn. I am going to go on further to find the rest. Once Shep has the cows in the barn, send him back to me," Daniel said, taking charge of the task.

William was all too glad to get to return to the barn with the cows and Shep. He knew that it was not the end of his day or the chores, but having to walk less than his brother pleased him.

Daniel walked on further out into the pasture. The land was not flat as people often thought of the plains. The landscape was rolling hills with trees dotting sparsely or in groves. There were plenty of places the other cows and horses could take shelter and remain hidden from the eye.

Seeing another group of cows, Daniel walked towards them, calling to the head cow. "Hey, cow! Come on, Bossy!"

Lifting her head from the grass upon which she was grazing, old Bossy started her slow meandering walk towards Daniel. The rest of the cows followed her lead. A well-worn path from the use by the cows for years was snaking back to the barn, and the old cow followed it habitually.

Daniel followed the cows for a short time but knew Old Bossy would lead the cows back to the barn. The cows' udders were filled with milk, and they would be uncomfortable until they were milked. The hay and the milking were incentive enough for the cows to follow blindly along.

Daniel was eager to find the horses. Forgetting to grab oat buckets and their halters, Daniel knew he was going to have a harder time getting them back to the barn. Standing on the top of a hill, Daniel looked down and saw all the horses grazing except Saul, who was on his back in a gully, struggling to get up.

Racing down the hill, Daniel yelled for Saul to get to his feet. The horse continued to struggle but could not get off his back onto his feet. Daniel knew the old horse had broken his leg.

Racing back to the farm, Daniel ran to the house. "Mama, I need the gun. Old Saul has broken his leg, and I have to put him out of his misery," Daniel said while trying hard to catch his breath.

Papa saw Daniel racing towards the house and ran after him. When hearing Daniel's story of Saul lying on his back, unable to get up, Papa took the rifle and asked Daniel to lead the way back to the horses. This time, Daniel quickly grabbed the halters and a bucket of oats that he neglected to take the first time.

Papa and Daniel walked quickly back to where Daniel said old Saul was down. Arriving at the top of the hill, Daniel saw all the horses grazing unconcernedly.

"But Papa, Saul was on his back and couldn't get up. I was sure he broke his leg," Daniel said, confused but also relieved.

Papa saw the lay of the land and remarked, "I think Saul decided to roll and got caught in that gully. He is old, and I suppose he just couldn't maneuver his body as well as he did in his younger years. Think of how hard it is for your grandpa to get up out of a deep sofa without help. Old Saul is no different than an old man. He doesn't have the muscles he once did."

Rattling the bucket of oats, all the horses' heads rose at hearing the familiar sound. The race for their favorite food was on, and

Papa and Daniel knew to be cautious as all four horses headed their way. Kicking and biting could follow as each horse tried to be the first to get the oats.

When Jack reached the bucket first, Daniel was ready with the halter and buckled it around his neck. Letting the pony get a mouthful of oats, Daniel pulled him away from the herd to put the halter on correctly, securing one of the horses, while Molly and Maud pushed and nipped at each other to be the second one to get oats. Saul moseyed up the hill where Daniel could easily halter him. The old horse knew that his master would make sure he got as many oats as the rest, so there was no hurry.

When all the horses were haltered and Saul got to lick the last oats from the bucket, Papa and Daniel led them back to the barn. All the cows were in their stalls waiting to be milked, while William threw down hay to keep the cows happy until the milking chores could be started.

Papa went from animal to animal to inspect for any cuts, bruises, or worse injuries that may have been received during the storm. All the herd appeared to be in good shape, with only a few cuts needing ointment. Papa said a silent prayer, thanking his Lord for any protection he provided for his family and his livestock.

CHAPTER NINE

At the breakfast table, Papa recalled hearing how the Indians said there never were tornadoes in this part of the country until the white man changed the course of the river.

"Do you think that is true, Papa," asked William. "When did the course of the river get changed?"

Papa shook his head, "I don't know about those things. I moved here with my father and mother. We came from Kentucky. Maybe the course of the river was different before we came here. I just am telling you what I heard. I don't know if any of it is true. I do know we have our fair share of tornadoes, though."

Mama scurried around the table, making sure everyone had enough to eat. There was plenty to do today, and she wanted to make sure her children had the energy to do what needed to be done.

"Abby, we have laundry to do today. I already have water on the stove heating so we can do the first load right after breakfast, Mama said before sitting down to eat.

"Oh, Mama! Do I really have to help? I can't reach the clothesline or anything. I want to play with the kittens," Abby whined.

"Abby," Mama said, "the boys are working out in the hot sun in the fields with your father. Everyone needs to help with this family.

You have chores to do, too. Just because you can't reach the clothesline does not mean that you can't hand me the wet clothes to hang. Would you rather weed the garden? You could do that instead, but it would be helpful if I did not need to bend down and pick up each and every item. Carrying baby George around all day long is hard on my back, and if you could save my back from that extra work, it sure would be nice."

"Okay, Mama," Abby agreed. "I will help you with the laundry. Besides, I don't know which sprout is a weed and which is a vegetable plant in the garden."

Abby smiled, thinking she got the better end of the deal. Her smile disappeared when Mama told her that she would show her the difference between an edible plant and a weed after they hung the laundry out to dry.

Gathering the dishes from the table and setting them on the small counter to be washed, the boys left with Papa to do the fieldwork. The corn and wheat were undamaged by the storm, but there was still weeding to do until the stalks grew so tall, they blocked the sun from the weeds. The shoots need protection from weeds and insects, so vigilance is required. The boys worked the fields since being Abby's age, so both knew what was expected of them.

Mama thanked the boys for helping to clear the table. She promised them a big meal at noon when they would return from the field to eat.

"What are you going to make?" Daniel asked, already hungry, just thinking about the next meal.

"It will be a surprise," Mama said, wanting to put a little mystery and fun into the day for her growing boys.

Walking out the screen door, Mama could hear William saying to his brother, "I bet Mama will make some of her canned beef for lunch with potatoes and gravy...." The slamming of the screen door blocked Mama from hearing Daniel's reply.

"Abby, you dry the dishes, and we will be done in just a matter of minutes," Mama said while handing Abby the dish towel. "Baby George should sleep for another hour before we need to feed, change, and entertain him. We will bring his cradle under the trees where we can hear him if he wakes up."

Before long, Mama had a large basket of clean clothes to hang on the line. Baby George woke up before Mama was able to carry the basket of laundry to the line outside. Breaking from her chores, Mama changed the baby and nursed him. Bringing a blanket to place under the tree, Mama asked Abby to sit with the baby while she hung the clothes to dry. Happily, Abby grabbed the rattle Papa made for the baby and sat under the tree, cooing and talking to her little brother.

Mama hauled the laundry basket out to the line. The clothes were extremely heavy once wet, and Mama arched her back to stretch it out once she set the heavy basket down on the ground. Taking time to rub the small of her back, Mama slowly reached down for the first item to hang on the line. Her apron was full of clothespins, and as she reached for the first one, she looked to the clear skies, thankful she would not need to contend with rain today.

Finally, Mama stepped back to watch her families' clothes fluttering in the wind. As the day warmed, Mama knew the clothes would dry quickly. Early afternoon, probably after the lunch dishes were done, she and Abby would be back out to the line to take the clothes down and fold them neatly for reuse.

Mama looked to the sun, wondering if she had time to weed the garden before starting lunch. The canned beef would be a quicker lunch than killing a chicken, plucking it, and cooking it. If she heated the canned meat, peeled and boiled some potatoes, and made gravy, she could possibly weed the garden first. Then Mama remembered she intended to make a simple cake for dessert. The weeding would need to wait.

"Abby, I need to go in and heat the stove to make a cake. Do you think you can stay with George a bit longer?" Mama asked.

"But Mama, I really need to pee. I want to go to the privy first," Abby answered.

Mama looked disgusted as she replied, "Abby, we don't use such a crude word. You need to go to the privy is sufficient. There is no reason a lady should use a word like 'pee.' Now scoot and hurry back."

Mama picked up the laundry basket and set it on the porch while watching the baby. Enjoying the freedom of lying on the blanket, baby George kicked his tiny little legs. The rattle was out of reach, and he seemed determined to get it back into his chubby little hands. Usually, the baby complained about being placed on his stomach, but his focus on the rattle seemed to cause him to forget how much he disliked the position.

Mama smiled while watching the newest member of the family. She thought it had not been that long ago when Abby was that small. She wondered how the years could go by so quickly. Daniel was as tall as many grown men, and William, though much smaller than his older brother, exhibited many traits that would serve him well as a man. Mama felt an enormous amount of pride, thinking about her children and imagined each as adults with families of their own.

Abby giggled as she ran back from the outhouse. "Mama, can I bring one of the kittens to play with while I watch George. He would love it!"

Mama was about to say no and that the kittens could have ringworms when she realized Abby was only four and needed something to do while she watched the baby. Minutes could feel like hours to a bored, small child. "Alright, but hurry, please. I have so much to do before our men return from the fields for lunch."

"Men? Only Papa is a man. Daniel and William are just boys," Abby said, correcting her mother.

"Just hurry, Abby," Mama said once more.

While keeping an eye on the baby, Mama opened the cellar doors. The canned meat was in the underground cellar. The cellar doubled as storage since the small kitchen pantry had little space. There was just enough room for everyday items in the kitchen pantry.

Seeing Abby return with one of the kittens, Mama descended the stairs with just enough sunlight coming down to light her way to the shelves Papa made to store goods.

Large and small mason jars lined the shelves. Mama grabbed two large jars of canned meat and one large jar of canned peaches. Mama decided the peaches would taste good on top of the simple cake she intended to bake. Carrying them back up the stairs, she set them down gently so she could close the two large doors to secure the cellar.

Abby was laughing as she teased the kitten with a long blade of grass. Baby George seemed amused and kicked gleefully, now on his back. Mama knew Abby would come running to the house if anything happened out of the ordinary.

Before long, it was noon, and Mama heard her husband telling Abby what a great babysitter she was, as he bent down to pick up the baby. William and Daniel were already at the pump washing the dirt off their hands, arms, and face from the hot, dirty work they performed that morning.

Taking the cake out of the oven to cool, Mama finished mashing the potatoes. The beef and gravy were hot and ready to serve. The vegetables in the cellar were diminishing after the long winter, so Mama was glad the garden would soon replenish her stores. Today, her family would need to be content without vegetables. However, the peaches would make up for the lack of anything green on their plates.

"See, I told you we would have canned beef, potatoes, and gravy, didn't I?" William hollered to Daniel as they entered the kitchen to sit at the table.

"It smells good, Lenora," Papa complimented his wife. Giving her a hug and a kiss before sitting down with the baby on his knee, Papa seemed happy with what he and the boys accomplished that morning.

"How are the crops?" Mama asked as she set the food on the table.

Smacking Daniel on the knuckles with the handle of his knife as Daniel reached for a bowl, Papa added, "I will tell you all about the crops after we say grace. Papa gave Daniel a stern look as he bowed his head to say a prayer of thanksgiving for the food they were about to eat.

Daniel sheepishly bowed his head as well while William smiled at his brother's discomfort. William rarely got in trouble with his parents, and he found it amusing that Daniel could not control his impulses and got in trouble frequently.

Before closing his eyes, Daniel shot William a fierce glare that meant to back off if William did not want to get punched later in the day. William immediately wiped the grin from his face, knowing he was about to face his older, larger brother's wrath.

All was forgotten as the boys dished up food upon their plates. Papa talked to Mama concerning the crops, the weather, and the usual small talk at the table.

Mama soon became aware of how much the boys were gobbling up and said, "Boys, I made dessert. If you overeat, you won't have room in your stomachs for the cake and peaches."

With food still in his mouth, Daniel mumbled, "Don't worry, Mama. I have room for cake and peaches."

"Daniel, if you continue to have such bad manners as talking with your mouth full, I think you might just skip dessert," Papa warned. "We chew, swallow, and then talk. No one wants to see the food in our mouths!"

"Sorry, Papa," Daniel said as he once again gave a warning glare to his younger brother to stop the grin forming on his lips.

"Clear the dishes from the table while your mama gets the dessert," Papa commanded.

Papa continued to bounce George on his knee while he finished up the last bit of potatoes and gravy on his plate. The canned beef was so tender, no one needed to use a knife, thus holding the baby was not difficult while Papa ate.

Savoring each bite of dessert, the boys ate slowly. The cake was gone, so there would be no seconds. That made it easier to eat slowly. Rushing would not get either of them a second portion of the cake. The few peaches remaining in the jar would be a snack for Abby later in the day as she ate very little at mealtimes.

Not in a rush, the boys sat and joined in on the conversations at the table. They both knew they would be returning to the fields to continue the hot work under the afternoon sun. Way before either boy was ready to continue the day's work, Papa was saying for the boys to get their hats to protect their heads from the sun and head out the door.

Mama knew she had much to do before she started the evening meal. Baby George would take a nap, and she and Abby would go into the garden to start weeding. First, the laundry needed to be put away. Handing Abby her stack of clothes, she told her to put them away neatly, as Mama climbed the stairs to the loft bedroom the boys shared.

The room was sparsely furnished. There was one bed and one dresser that the boys shared. A crudely made armoire that Papa built by hand for the boys to hang their church clothes and coats was crammed in the corner of the room. William stacked books neatly under the window, but no pictures were adorning the walls or scattered toys on the floor. The boys possessed few toys, and what they owned, they shared. There was one sled for the winter when snow was on the ground, but it was stored in the barn. A deck of cards was in the sitting room for the whole family to play games on nights when they did not need to go to bed early. Mama spied the bat and ball that the boys received the past year at Christmas, placed in one corner. Other than those few items, the room was bare but clean.

Mama looked at the bed. She sat many months sewing the squares of material into a quilt for the boys' bed. Smiling, she was pleased the boys pulled it up to make their room neat before going out to do the morning chores. She wondered whether the two boys made the bed together or if William made the bed alone. She wanted to think it was a joint effort.

Closing the bedroom door, Mama returned downstairs. George would sleep for two hours, and that would give her and Abby plenty of time in the garden. Mama knew Abby could recognize a weed from a vegetable plant but was glad to have the excuse to spend time with her daughter doing the chore, pretending to give her a lesson.

Grabbing gloves and a hoe, Mama and Abby went out to the garden. The kitten was no longer in sight. Mama knew the Mama cat retrieved her kitten while the family ate their noon meal. She watched from the window as she served the meal when it happened.

"Mama, I don't like turnips. Why do you grow them in the garden?" Abby asked as her little fingers grabbed one weed after another.

Mama continued to hoe while she thought about an answer. Stopping the back-breaking work for a second, Mama rubbed her back and stretched.

"Abby, turnips are incredible," Mama finally said. "We can eat the greens, and we can eat the root. Nothing is wasted. The turnip is good for your stomach. Even if it does not taste sweet like carrots, it has many vitamins that your little body needs to grow big and strong. I want you to think of turnips as your body's best friend next time you eat one."

Aghast, Abby questioned, "Why would I want to eat my best friend?"

Mama just smiled at her daughter and continued working in the garden. She thought about the fresh vegetables she would serve her family and all the work it would take to can some of them to last the winter. Others would store nicely in the cellar for future meals, but if her crop of vegetables were eaten by insects or damaged by hail, there would not be enough to make it until next year. She hated to think about having to spend the money at the store to buy vegetables if she ran out.

Hearing baby George crying, Mama announced that they would stop for now. "George needs us to come into the house. I will change him and feed him, and then I will need you to entertain George while I start dinner. Thank you for being such a good big sister, Abby. I can always count on you."

Mama added those last words when she saw Abby start to make a face. Mama knew the next words out of her daughter's mouth would be complaints about how she always has to babysit.

Instead of grumbling, Abby beamed at her mother's praise and skipped happily into the house to help entertain her baby brother. While Mama fed and changed the baby, Abby looked around for his rattle. Not finding it, Abby grabbed her dolly and decided she could use her toy like a puppet.

Mama left baby George lying on a blanket while Abby told a story about how her dolly was a princess from a faraway country.

Smiling, realizing her daughter's imagination was one of her best resources, Mama turned her thoughts to dinner preparation.

CHAPTER TEN

Summer wasn't all work for the boys. Daniel worked extra hours to help Mr. Mueller as promised, but there was still time to go fishing with William. Mama always welcomed having something new to cook for the family other than beef, pork, or chicken. Fish from the pond, or river when Papa went along, was a treat for the family.

"There is still plenty of sunlight left in the day. Papa, can William and I go to the pond and fish?" Daniel asked, hoping his father wouldn't notice the leather harnesses needed to be cleaned with linseed oil.

Papa followed Daniel's eyes to the harnesses. "I suppose you two deserve a break. I will clean those harnesses for you so you can fish," Papa said, smiling.

Feeling guilty, Daniel added, "If we all clean the harnesses, we can get the job done quickly, and then maybe you can come fishing with us."

"That would be nice, but I promised your mother that I would do some of my honey-do chores. It won't take me long to clean the harnesses. You two go along, but be careful. I don't want your mother to need to do more laundry because one of you sank into the mud or fell into the pond."

Rushing to grab the bamboo fishing poles and old wooden tackle box, the boys promised they would be careful and ran off to the pond. Papa watched them with pride, and with a bit of regret that he could not go along.

"I will race you to the pond," shouted Daniel as he grabbed his bobbers, hooks, and a hand trowel to dig for worms.

"No fair! You have longer legs. You know I can't keep up with you," William cried back.

Daniel slackened his pace and allowed his younger brother to catch up with him. "Mama said the church is having an ice cream social on Sunday. I can't wait. I guess Mama is going to help make the ice cream. She makes the best strawberry ice cream ever. I am glad Papa bought strawberry plants for Mama several years ago."

"Yeah, but when Mama asks you to go out and pick the strawberries for the ice cream, don't eat all the best ones," William reprimanded, knowing Daniel's propensity for anything sweet.

"Why don't you offer to pick the strawberries, and then you won't have to worry about my getting the best ones?" asked Daniel.

"I just might do that!" shot back William, not realizing that Daniel just tricked him into doing the work of picking strawberries.

Letting the subject drop before William started to realize how much bending down was required to pick strawberries, Daniel turned the conversation back to fishing.

"Maybe we won't have to dig for worms. I noticed a few grasshoppers around yesterday. They should do well as bait if we can catch some," suggested Daniel.

William looked at his brother. "You know fish like worms or minnows the best. I don't want to spend time chasing grasshoppers when we can net some minnows and use them. We can always use our imitation frogs, too."

"If I see any grasshoppers on the way, I am going to catch them. I think the bass would like to eat them. Maybe the bluegill would like a change of diet, too," Daniel said as he kept a close eye on the grass for any movement.

Finally, reaching the best spot on the pond, Daniel sat down under the one lonely tree that shaded the pond. Most of the trees were cleared years ago for farming, but since this section of land was for grazing the cattle, a few oak trees spotted the landscape to provide shade during the hottest time of the year. The boys set their gear down and baited the hooks with the imitation frogs.

"We can start with the frogs until we catch some minnows or dig up a few worms," William said as he threw his line out into the pond. The red and white bobber merrily danced upon the surface movement of the water, ready to announce any strike a fish might make.

Daniel threw his line out as far as he could throw it. "You see if you can net some minnows, and I will watch our bobbers to make sure we don't miss a strike."

William grumbled, knowing he was being left with the work of finding bait while his brother sat under the shade tree and did nothing.

"I am not sharing my bait with you. You are lazy, and I don't appreciate it," grumbled William.

"I am not lazy," Daniel retaliated. "If a fish strikes and no one is here to pull the fish out, we will lose it. I am a responsible fisherman."

On cue, one of the bobbers sank beneath the surface of the water. Daniel clumsily sprang to his feet to grab the pole planted into the dirt. As he reached for the pole, it started to take off toward the water. Daniel needed to jump forward to grab the pole, landing on his belly. He quickly grabbed the end of the pole, pulling the pole back sharply to make sure the hook was set. Daniel was delighted to feel the heavy tug, tug, tug on the line. The fish was on the hook. Now the battle would begin.

Daniel got to his feet and realized this was a huge fish. He grabbed the butt end of the pole with his left hand and with his right hand, he grabbed above the middle of the pole.

William was surprised to see just how much fight was left in the fish and how much tugging it was doing. He asked Daniel, "What do you think it is? A catfish or a bass?"

Daniel responded in a high pitched, excited voice, "Don't think it is a catfish. It ain't pulling, it is tugging. It must be a bass—a big bass!"

"Don't pull so much. Let it fight the tip just like Papa always says," William instructed.

"If I don't pull back some, it will pull me into the water. I am going to try to tire it out. Maybe I will let it tug itself until it quits," Daniel countered.

Just then, the fish decided to take a right turn and run directly towards Daniel and the shore. Daniel quickly backed up, keeping the line taut.

William encouraged, "Good job! Keep fighting, Daniel."

The bass took a mighty leap out of the water and revealed itself. Daniel, with his mouth wide open, almost dropped the pole.

William let out a hoot. "That is not a big fish; that is a giant fish. You just caught Old Grandpa! Don't lose it."

Daniel continued to fight the line, and he could tell the fish was tiring, especially after the one big jump. Daniel's adrenalin was waning, and he could feel his body beginning to fatigue, just like Old Grandpa. Just then, to his surprise, Old Grandpa starts tugging more than ever.

"William, I think Old Grandpa isn't ready to die." Daniel continued, "I am wondering whether I should let him go. He has been the king of this pond for many years. I kinda hate to be the one to end his reign. Just consider how many other basses in this pond he has fathered."

Being tender-hearted, William pondered what his brother said and agreed. "Yes, let the old fish live to father more bass. We don't want to overfish this pond anyway."

"I still need to bring him in to take the hook out. I want to see how big he is anyway." Daniel continued with a request, "Get that string out of the tackle box so we can measure how fat he is and how long this monster is. Papa won't believe us otherwise."

As Daniel continued to gently draw the fish towards the shore, William arrived with the spool of string and a knife. Wading into the shallows so the fish would not be out of the water, Daniel held the fish by his largemouth while William measured its length, cutting the string precisely at the end of its tail. Wrapping another length of string around his belly, William cut that piece and placed it in his right pocket. William gave the other line to Daniel so they would not lose track of which string was the length and which was the girth.

Removing the hook from the largemouth bass, Daniel reached under its belly and hoisted it once in the air and screamed, "Dang! This is one heavy fish."

Slowly, he held the fish by the tail and moved it back and forth in the water to revive it. Once the fish was showing signs of life, Daniel let go and watched his trophy fish swim away to live another day.

With surprise, Old Grandpa made one last jump—the highest jump yet to show his appreciation and to say good-bye. With a flick of a tail, he somersaulted back into the water and disappeared into the depths.

Being too excited to continue fishing, the boys gathered their gear and raced back home to show Papa the size of the fish they released. Yelling for Papa as they approached the house, they were greeted by their father on the porch.

"What is all the ruckus about?" Papa asked, seeing his red-faced boys approaching.

"Daniel caught Old Grandpa!" William said with glee.

Papa looked for the old fish and puzzled at not seeing a fish, said, "Where is the fish""

Daniel said excitedly, "We let him go, but he was a giant. Look, we measured the fish with string. Papa, where is the ruler, so we can see how big he really was."

Papa looked at the two lengths of strings the boys each held up in their hands. Papa wondered why each was holding one.

"This one is how long the fish was," William said, pointing to the length of the string in Daniel's hand, "and the one I have was the fish's girth."

"Wow!" Papa declared. "That looks like a huge fish. I will get the ruler, and we will see just how big Old Grandpa really is. We will go into the barn and carve the length and girth as well as the date you caught him, so if we catch him again, we can see how much bigger he is getting."

With the ruler in hand and the two lengths of string, the three raced off to the barn to find the perfect beam to carve their catch. Papa announced the fish was 22 inches long and the girth was 24 inches, proving the fish possessed a large bucket belly full of food.

"That is a good sign that our pond is healthy. There seems to be plenty of food for the fish. How heavy do you think the fish was?" Papa asked, knowing this was an excellent time to teach the boys an old trick to determine a fish's weight.

Daniel said, "He was heavy, Papa. I could barely hold him out of the water."

"Okay, we know how long he was and what his girth was. You think you can calculate in your head, or do you need paper and a pencil?" Papa asked.

William proudly announced, "I can figure in my head, Papa. What do I need to do?"

"Well first, you need to multiply the girth times the girth. So, what are 24 times 24?"

Almost instantly, William announces the answer is 576.

"Now, you must multiply 576 by the length, which is 22 inches," challenged Papa.

William took several seconds to think through the arithmetic and declared that he knew the answer.

"Papa, if I have done the calculation right in my head, the number is huge. It is 12,672."

Daniel stood by with amazement as his younger brother announced the number. "Wow! I didn't know I could lift anything that heavy," Daniel beamed.

Papa laughed, "We aren't finished with our arithmetic. William, we need to divide that number by 800, and that should give us the weight of Old Grandpa."

This time, William knew 8 would go into 12 one time, so the arithmetic was not as hard as he thought it might be. Daniel, with a stick in his hand, scratched the numbers into the dirt of the barn floor, seeing if he could beat William with the answer.

"The answer is 15.84 pounds, Papa," William said before Daniel got half of the answer written in the dirt.

"Gosh, that isn't near as heavy as I thought when I lifted the fish high out of the water," Daniel said disappointedly.

"That is larger than any bass I have ever caught," Papa said with pride. "Maybe it is even larger than any caught in the state.

Probably bigger than any caught in this here United States. Unfortunately, our state does not keep any records. You need to keep this quiet, or we will have people trespassing on our property to catch Old Grandpa. You are a good fisherman, son, but you can't brag about it. Understand?"

Daniel thought about someone else catching Old Grandpa and didn't like the idea at all. He decided right then and there that no one would ever find out how big his fish was on this very special day.

"Papa, I promise not to tell anyone. I couldn't stand the thought of someone else catching and keeping Old Grandpa. He is my fish, and that is his pond, and no one else is ever going to take him from his home. I can tell Mama, though, can't I?"

"Yes, son, you can tell your mama. Go ahead. You have the bragging rights to do that much," Papa said as he watched Daniel sprint from the barn.

"Mama," Daniel was heard shouting as he raced to the screen door.

Papa turned to William. "You did the calculations; you should be the one to carve the weight into the beam. I am proud of you, boy."

Walking into the house from leaving the barn, Papa and William heard Daniel telling his mother, "The fish was 35 inches long...right?" Daniel asked, turning to his brother and father for confirmation as he held his hands wide apart.

Mama chuckled, knowing how many fishermen exaggerated the size of any big fish they caught. "Really?" Mama said.

CHAPTER ELEVEN

Hot and humid was the only words to describe the summer on the plains. Working out in the sun was exhausting. Sweat being wiped from eyes was a common occurrence from the moment the guys got out in the field until they got back home. Washing up at the end of the workday was not only necessary but a luxury.

"Tonight, you will need to bathe. We are going to the ice cream social at church," Mama said as she poked her head out of the screen door where the boys were washing up at the pump.

Daniel was about to object to having to thoroughly bathe until he heard the ice cream social part of the deal. As Mama's head pulled back into the darkness of the parlor, Daniel nudged his little brother.

"Ice cream! I can't wait. This is going to be so much fun. Some of our schoolmates will be there, and we can catch up with what is going on with them," Daniel said.

William snickered, "You mean catching up with Becky, don't you?"

Daniel scooped up a double handful of water and threw it into William's face. "Take that, you squid!"

William responded in kind and hurled water back at his big brother. Whoops and laughter filled the yard until Papa slammed the screen door behind him.

"Boys! Knock that off right now. You are both dripping wet. You are not coming in for dinner and tracking all over the floor. You can just sit out here until you dry."

"Now look what you got us into," snarled William. "We probably won't get any dinner!"

"Stop crying like a big baby," snapped back Daniel. "It won't hurt you to miss one little meal. You are getting pudgy anyway."

"Who are you calling pudgy?" yelled William jumping to his feet and making a fist.

"Boys, if you can sit down quietly and stop your fighting, I will pass out plates of food for you to eat," Mama said from behind the dusty screen door.

Daniel jumped to his feet to open the screen door, which he noticed for the first time, required repairs. Seeing the holes large enough for flies to enter, Daniel wondered why Mama had not asked Papa to replace the screen months ago.

Taking both plates from his Mama's outstretched hands, Daniel smiled gratefully and thanked his mother. "I knew you wouldn't let your growing boys go without food."

"Just eat and bring the dishes back inside when you are dry enough to come into the house," Mama said before returning into the shadows of the house.

William took one of the plates and sat down, forgetting the mean thing his brother said to him only seconds earlier. He couldn't decide which to eat first, his drumstick from a chicken or the corn on the cob. He knew the early corn would be sweet and delicious, but Mama's fried chicken was the best in the world. Grabbing the chicken leg, William tore into the crisp outer crust of breadcrumbs and flour with which his mother always dredged the chicken.

"Mama's chicken is the best in the world!" William said as he chewed. "No one can fry chicken like Mama."

Daniel did not answer, but only nodded his head. He, too, was biting and chewing with gusto. Taking the corn on the cob, Daniel ate the entire thing in one sitting. Seeing the chickens scratching around the yard for bugs and seeds, Daniel tossed the cobb knowing the chickens would relish the few leftover corns on the cob.

Daniel was right. The chickens flocked to the cob, pecking the leftovers with delight. One hen managed to peck out an entire corn kernel and raced off with two other hens pursuing. The game of chase was on.

Daniel remarked that they should start a similar game at the ice cream social. "If we can get our hands on a ball, we can play keep-away or some other game. It would be fun since we have that huge yard and the cemetery at the back of the church."

"I don't think the pastor will let us run around the cemetery. He thinks we should be solemn whenever we approach the gates to the cemetery. Using it to play *hide-and-seek* or any other game would offend his sensibilities."

Daniel yawned, acting bored with his little brother's vocabulary and the use of such a big word. "I am sure the pastor has better things to do with his sensibilities, don't you think?"

"You don't even know what the word means, so why are you even pretending to know?" challenged William.

"I do, too, know what it means," corrected Daniel.

"Okay, smarty-pants, what do sensibilities mean?" continued William's challenge.

"It means the pastor can see and smell if we are out in the cemetery, so there!" Daniel said smugly.

"That is ridiculous!" answered William. "It means no such thing. It means if you must know, that the pastor has a good perception as to what other peoples' emotions may be. He would know that the Widow Charlotte would be offended if we were using her dead husband's grave as a playground. That is what it means, Dumbbell."

"Perceptions? What does that mean?" asked Daniel, stopping the conversation in its tracks.

"Forget it. Just use your brawn. Your mind is hopeless," William said, dishing out more insults.

Daniel was just about ready to pummel his little brother for the remarks when Papa once again came to the screen door.

"Boys, you have chores to finish. Hand me your plates. I don't want to hear any more fighting or insults. If I need to intervene, you won't like it. I expect the two of you to work together. Maybe both of you should refrain from talking to each other until after church tomorrow. I suggest you pray for guidance on how you can treat your brother as a member of God's Kingdom."

Sadly, Papa took the plates and looked at each of his sons. Giving a long warning look to each, Papa turned without another word. The boys felt his disappointment, and it made each feel horrible. Neither of them wanted to be a disappointment to their father.

Racing to the barn, not a word was said as the cows were given hay to keep them occupied while the milking chores were being completed. Each boy had the same number of cows to milk. Daniel usually finished first since his hands were larger and stronger, but William could keep pace with his quickness and gentle touch. Today, William fell behind, and Daniel took his pail to milk the remaining cow that was William's to do.

Papa came into the barn to do chores of his own and noted that Daniel was helping his younger brother to complete his task. Papa wanted to compliment his older son for being charitable but knew William would resent any comment made at this time. Papa kept quiet and went about his work.

Daniel may not have the ability to excel in schoolwork like William, but Papa knew his older son was not stupid. He was smart in many ways, especially farming. Daniel knew animals and what they needed. He could do a man's work, and he could think through hard tasks to get them completed. He just didn't have the most extensive vocabulary, nor could he calculate in his head like William, but he could get the answer with paper and pencil. Daniel could always get the task done. That is what counted in this world.

William, Papa knew, felt intimidated by his older brother's natural abilities and strengths. Papa wondered if he did not give William enough praise for the things he did well, so William would not need to compete with Daniel on grounds he could not compete. There was no way William would ever be as strong or large as Daniel. William knew he would need to rely on his brain and quick wit. Papa knew those traits would also serve his younger son well.

Turning his thoughts to baby George, Papa had no idea what kind of man he may turn out to be. At this point, all Papa knew for sure that his baby son possessed a pleasant temperament. He hardly ever cried and was easily soothed when he did get hurt or was uncomfortable. He smiled and laughed easily. Charming was the word that popped into Papa's mind. 'Little Prince Charming' thought Papa as he went up into the hayloft to throw down more hay for the cows' breakfast.

While in the loft, Papa checked on the birds that Daniel and William were raising to sell. Papa saw there was fresh water and plenty of seeds for the birds, and he knew immediately that William and Daniel had taken care of the birds earlier that afternoon. Soon many of the birds would weigh enough to take to the store. It was not much money, but every little bit helped to pay the remainder of the hospital bills.

Below, the boys were gathering the hay that Papa tossed down. The chores were automatically done, like a well-greased machine. The boys and Papa had been working side by side for years now. Each knew what was expected of them. When the boys were not sparing, they worked together like a *well-greased machine*. Looking down from the loft, Papa beamed and yelled down to the boys, "Good job, boys. I am proud of how well you are working together."

Mama placed berry pie on the table when the boys came in from the barn. The temptation to grab a piece was tempered only by the sight of seeing the preparation of the ritual Saturday evening baths.

The wood-burning stove held every pot and pan available filled with water. Once heated, the water would serve to warm the tub water so each child could bath. Mama knew she would be refilling each pot or pan many times to get all of the children bathed before bed. This was the typical Saturday evening habit—soaking to be clean for Sunday church.

Baby George and Abby were already bathed and in their pajamas. Abby rocked baby George and sang songs to him as he kicked his little legs in delight.

"Who is first?" Mama asked as the boys finished their pie.

The boys knew that whoever bathed first got the cleaner water, so it was always a fight. The next boys would sit in the other boy's bathwater, and even though more hot water was added, each boy hated to sit in the used water, knowing what they knew about each other.

"I am first!" shouted Daniel. "The last time I was the second man in, William peed in the water just to make me mad."

"That is not true. I did not pee in the water," William said, rather unconvincingly.

"I don't want to hear either of you talking like that!" Mama said without humor. "It is not funny. If I find out either of you is urinating in the bathwater, you will not be laughing when Papa gets finished with you. We are civilized humans in this house. We are not crude animals!"

Seeing fire in her eyes, there was no doubt that Mama was mad. She brought a steaming hot kettle of water to the tub. "Daniel, if you are first, get two buckets of water and place them in the tub to cool down the boiling water. You best strip out of your clothes and get into the tub before the water cools off too much. Scrub yourself with soap, and I will bring rinse water. Hurry, though, I want William in and out of the tub before your father arrives. He needs to be next after you, boys, and we will need to drain the tub before he gets in."

"Why does Papa always get fresh water, and Daniel and I have to bathe in used bathwater?" William said at his own risk.

Daniel knew William was acting foolish to ask that question when Mama was in a bad mood due to finding out her boys would pee in the bathwater. Daniel whispered, "Let it go, William. You are treading on eggshells right now."

It was too late. Mama heard William's question, and she had an answer.

"Your papa deserves freshwater because he is the man of this house. He is the reason we all have food on our plates and a roof over our heads. Without your papa, you would need to live on the streets and beg like street urchins. That is why your father gets fresh water for every bath he takes," Mama said with her voice rising to a shrill pitch.

William shut up and helped Daniel bring in the buckets of water, while Mama stomped off to the kitchen to retrieve more hot water.

"Whew, you really stepped in it that time," Daniel said quietly to his brother.

"You can say that again. I guess I will just have to take extra time to wash the s h i t off my feet." William whispered as both boys broke out into laughter.

The next morning found the Dolen family scrubbed and clean, wearing their best clothes to go to church. Mama suggested the boys take a change of clothes if they planned to play with the other children after church. She was not about to have their best clothes soiled or torn due to careless play.

The team was hitched and ready for the family to step up into the wagon. Papa drove, and Mama sat with baby George in her arms, with Abby tucked in on the hard seat between herself and Papa. The boys rode in the back, making sure they found the cleanest spot to sit. Blankets or straw were usually left in the back to provide some comfort for the ones who did not have a seat up front.

"Papa, when are we going to get an automobile?" Daniel asked.

"I am afraid we need a tractor before we get an automobile. We will need to see how well the crops sell before I can answer your question. Our team is getting older. I doubt they have too many years left where they can pull the plow or this wagon, for that matter."

Daniel let the question stay unanswered. He knew there were too many variables in farming. The weather was either friend or foe. Insects and other blights always plagued the farmer as well. Gamblers were what many people called farmers. The odds of having a good crop depended on so much. Then, if everyone managed a good harvest, there was too much competition, and that was just as bad as having too little to sell. Finding buyers and getting a fair price wasn't easy, either. Daniel loved farming, but he wondered whether a more secure job might be a better route for him to take. He knew William would not stay on the farm once he graduated from high school. William was already talking about wanting to work for the newspaper where he could write stories.

Daniel knew he wanted to work outdoors. There is no way he could work in a building all day long, sitting down. That would drive him crazy. He needed to use his body and his strength. It felt good to build something with wood or metal and work hard physically. Building things...carpentry work or construction work might be the answer.

The church was in sight. Daniel continued to let his thoughts bounce around his head while sitting in the pews. The pastor talked too long, and Daniel did not hear a word. When he wasn't thinking about building the next biggest building, he was sneaking a look at Becky.

Becky wasn't as pretty as Ellie, the storekeeper's daughter, but Becky was cute. Her hair was brown, but a shiny brown with bits of gold-flecked strands interspersed in her hair. When Becky wore her hair in braids, the colors mingled back and forth through each intricate pattern where the bright hair peeked and poked through the interlacing of the dominant brown hair. It was like spying treasures of gold just within reach.

William's elbow slammed into Daniel's ribs. "Stop mooning over Becky," William said in a stage whisper.

Mama's eyes locked onto William's eyes in one second with a sharp warning that he'd better stop talking in the church if he wanted any ice cream. William knew that look and stopped talking immediately. William knew Mama would make sure he did not get any of her strawberry ice cream if he said one more word. Relieved when the congregation started to sing, William took one more chance to tease his brother, "Becky only has eyes for Henry, anyway."

Daniel glared at William. He was about to say something when he saw his mother turn her head in his direction. He immediately broke out in a loud version of 'A Mighty Fortress is Our God.' Embarrassed by Daniel's brash singing voice, Mama signaled for Daniel to bring down the noise level to blend in with the rest of the congregation.

Running out to change their clothes so they could play after having a sandwich and some ice cream, the boys quickly changed on the far side of the wagon, hoping no one would see them stepping out of their trousers before putting on their jeans. Folding their Sunday clothes nicely and putting them on the blanket in the back of the wagon, they once again raced to find their friends.

The parents brought their hand-cranked ice cream makers and set them outside the back door of the church. Each family boasted having the best recipe for ice cream, so a friendly competition was set up to benefit the church. Each member paid to taste the different ice creams. Extra coins were placed in the bowl of the ice cream they felt was the best. The church received all the money cast as votes.

Each family who competed must provide their own ice cream freezer, ice, and salt for the outer chamber, and cream, sugar, and a flavoring for the inner chamber where the delicious ice cream would be formed. The process took some time since churning by hand was hard work.

Daniel knew he would be called, at some point, from his play to take his turn at cranking the handle to churn the mixture. He would play as hard as he could until he heard his father's familiar whistle telling him to stop everything and come running.

Earlier that morning, Daniel went to the ice house to retrieve enough ice, leftover from the winter when it was cut from the frozen river. By summer, most of the ice had been used or melted. However, stored in the ice house insulated by straw, some ice always remained throughout the summer. Ice, sugar, and salt, much in demand, made ice cream expensive but the best treat imaginable.

Mama used strawberries to make her ice cream even sweeter than the plain vanilla ice cream. Mama started with hot cream to ensure the sugar crystals would be dissolved, egg yolks, and vanilla bean seeds were added. Each housewife possessed a secret family recipe that came with bragging rights for decades. Picking a winner, varied from year to year as each housewife made changes to her own family recipe. Some years the changes made the ice cream better, but not always.

Daniel thought about the year Mrs. Granger added elderberries to her recipe. Not realizing the berries needed to be cooked before eating, Mrs. Granger added fresh berries to her ice cream mixture. Many people who ate her ice cream ended up rushing to the outhouses in the churchyard. Daniel laughed to himself at the memory of people dancing in line and pounding on the outhouse door for the occupant to hurry. Since he was not one of the people who ate her ice cream, he could laugh. He vowed to check to see what kind of ice cream Mrs. Granger was making today. Daniel hoped she would stick to making cookies or cakes since she was particularly good at baking.

On cue, Papa whistled for Daniel to take his turn at churning the ice cream. Papa completed the easy work, so Daniel believed since the paddle plowed slowly through the cream mixture with difficulty.

Having the last time slot for churning was difficult, true, but it had its reward. It meant that Daniel would be first in line to taste his mother's strawberry ice cream. That made it worth the hard work. He knew Mama would not make him pay a nickel for a small bowl of ice cream since he put in some much muscle power to make the ice cream happen.

Daniel's pocket held several nickels so that he could sample several other bowls of ice cream. He knew he would put in a nickel coin into his mother's dish to give her a head start in winning the prize. It was bragging rights only, but Mama would blush and be modest while bursting with pride inside. Daniel wanted to see his mama, happy.

As the children spread out to taste ice cream, Daniel made a choice to have another bowl of his mother's strawberry ice cream. Putting all his nickels into her dish, he held out his bowl for another sample.

"Daniel, if you put all your nickels in my dish, you won't get to sample anyone else's ice cream. There could be a flavor out there you have never tried that you might like better than my strawberry," Mama told her son.

"Mama, I know I like your strawberry ice cream," Daniel said. "Why would I want to take a chance of getting a bowl of elderberry ice cream when I know your ice cream won't send me to the privy?" Daniel said with a wink. Mama filled Daniel's bowl to the brim and winked back.

The church raised over forty dollars from the ice cream social, and everyone had a good time. Mama came away with bragging rights for the third year in a row. Daniel came away with a full stomach and a full heart.

CHAPTER TWELVE

Harvest time was a time of excitement, even though it was lots of hard work. Daniel was working for the family farm as well as helping Mr. Mueller to repay his debt when his horse ran afoul in Mr. Mueller's field. The school year would not start until harvesting the crops was completed as most of the children were involved in some capacity on their family farm. What crops that the family could not harvest by themselves required teams of neighboring farmers to complete.

"The threshing crew may come anytime today or tomorrow, Abby. I am going to need you to help as much as you can. If you can keep your baby brother entertained, it will help me a lot. I will have as many as twenty men to feed. I have asked Papa to bring in a couple roasts. That way, if they come to the house, I can slice it and serve it with potatoes, vegetables, and fruit. If they are planning on eating in the field, I will need to make two sandwiches a piece for them," Mama said while peeling potatoes and covering them with water to keep them from turning brown.

Abby stopped what she was doing as she watched how anxious her mother was acting. "It isn't fair that you have to feed all those men, Mama," Abby said with a pout.

"It would sure be hard on your father and brothers to have to do all the extra work that the machines can do. Since Mr. Stevens has a tractor and a combine machine, he can do the work so much faster with the help of all the other men in the area. If the team of men goes from farm to farm, the extra hands make the work so much easier. Having to feed all those men for one or two days isn't such a bad deal, now is it?" Mama said in the way of an answer.

Abby went back to her chore of helping to peel the potatoes. "What about all our fruit being eaten. I picked apples until my back was aching. I sure don't want to see all my apples eaten in one day."

Mama smiled, knowing how much Abby loved eating fruit. If the men were to eat all the turnips or carrots, Abby would not be upset.

"Abby, we have lots of apples yet to pick. I want to thank you for picking all the apples that fell to the ground. You saved my back a lot of strain. We are a good team. I climb the ladder and pick the apples high in the tree, and you pick all the apples on the ground," Mama said. "I think we will make applesauce cookies to take out to the men if they eat in the field. It would be easier than making pies."

Abby thought for a moment, "But that means we will need to cook the apples and then mash them. It might be easier just to put them in a pie."

"Well, we might make individual pies for them. Would you help me make turnovers? That way, each man can have a dessert, and it would be easy to pack in the baskets we will use to carry out the meal," Mama said as she contemplated the menu.

The screen door slammed as William and Daniel entered the house. Papa sent the boys home to make sure Mama didn't need any help before they went back to the field to continue picking corn.

The corn was planted in the spring with forty-two inches between rows so the horses could get between the cornstalks when it was fully grown. Papa told the boys when they could afford a tractor that they would plant corn thirty inches between the rows so they could get a lot more corn to grow, which would mean more money.

At this point, the corn was picked and shucked by hand. The wagon loads of corn were taken to Mr. Mueller, who owned a mechanized corn sheller. They paid Mr. Mueller, but it sure made the work easier than trying to get the kernels off of the cob by hand.

"Papa sent us home to pick up lunch, and to see if you need help with anything before, we go back out into the field," William shouted upon entering the kitchen.

Mama knew that Papa was giving the boys a rest from the back-breaking work. She wanted to send something special in Papa's lunch for being so thoughtful of the children.

"How about if you boys go out and pick a bushel more apples for me. Abby and I are going to make apple turnovers for the threshing crew, but it will take every apple we picked to make enough. While you two are doing that chore, I will make some Kool-Aid for you to take out for lunch with your sandwiches."

"Kool-Aid!" Daniel repeated with enthusiasm. "I love Kool-Aid. I will pick every apple on the whole apple tree for Kool-Aid."

"A bushel will do, Daniel. Maybe later, I will need help picking the rest of the orchard, but not today. We have way too much work to do to get ready for tomorrow's workload," Mama said with a grin on her lips.

The door slammed loudly, announcing the boys had left the house to pick the apples Mama requested. Mama quickly packed the sandwiches into the basket and filled quart jars with the cold Kool-Aid. The fresh bread from the oven was cut thickly to make a filling sandwich. Both peanut butter and sliced sweet pickles, as well as meat sandwiches, filled the basket.

Mama looked at the bread dough that was rising. She would need to make many loaves of bread for the men who would descend on their farm tomorrow. Thankfully, Mrs. Mueller and Mrs. Granger said they would come to help her prepare the meals for the men. Mama knew it would take more than one day at each farm to thresh all the grain each farmer had waiting.

For days the boys and Papa cut the grain stems, making bundles called sheaves. Arranging the bundles, the boys shocked the bundles into an A-shaped conical shock that looked like tipis. These sheaves left to dry for days would be fed into the threshing machine tomorrow.

Abby asked if she could watch as the sheaves were fed into the machine. Papa explained how the threshing machine worked to her the night before, and Abby now thought she was an expert.

"Mama, Papa told me the shocks would be fed into the machine. The gears beat the wheat and make the kernels separate from the stalks. Then, Mama, a conveyor belt moves the wheat kernels into the hopper below. The stalks come out and become the straw that we use for bedding for the animals." Abby took a deep breath and continued where she left off. "After that, the auger moves the grain from the hopper to the sifting area. It gets sifted twice to remove all the dust and small particles, and finally, the auger moves the grain up to the spout that dumps the grain into a wagon so it can go to market."

Beaming with pride that she could repeat what Papa told her as well as panting for air from her non-stop monologue, Abby looked to her mother for praise. Seeing that Mama was barely listening as she folded the bread dough over on the counter, Abby found herself getting frustrated.

"Mama! Did you listen to a word I said?" Abby said in a scolding tone of voice.

Mama nodded her head, "Yes, Honey, I heard every word. You are an amazing little girl. I bet your brothers could not explain the process as well as you, and you have never even seen the machine."

"So, can I go out and watch tomorrow? I want to see the machine," Abby said excitedly, forgiving her mother for not being as attentive as she thought she should have been.

Mama stopped working for a moment. "Abby, the field with all those men, horses, wagons, and machines is no place for a little girl. However," Mama said before Abby could protest, "you can go with me when I take the lunch out to the men. They will still be working when we get there, so you will be able to see the machine in action. How is that?"

Abby seemed perfectly fine with what her mother was offering as a solution until she remembered her baby brother. At the moment, George was sleeping, but Abby knew the baby could not be left home alone.

"What about George? Will we take him out to the field? He is too small to be around all those men, horses, wagons, and that threshing machine," Abby said, acting like an adult.

Trying to ease Abby's fears, Mama said, "I am sure Mrs. Granger will be delighted to stay with George while we deliver lunch," Mama continued. "I think it was very mature of you to be aware of the dangers for your little brother. You are going to be a perfect mother someday."

The boys returned with the apples and grabbed the lunch basket, and were off before Mama could thank them for picking the fruit.

"Well, that was a fine howdy-do. I didn't even get to thank your brothers for picking the apples before they were gone," Mama said while blinking her eyes in disbelief that the boys didn't even have the good manners to say goodbye or thank you.

"The boys don't expect a thank you for doing the chores they are expected to do because they are part of this family," Abby said, once more sounding just like her mother.

Mama started to wonder if she really sounded like that. 'I can't be that bossy, can I?'

On the following day, morning came early. Everyone was up before the crack of dawn. The crew could be at their house very soon or by late afternoon. Chores needed to be completed early so that Papa and the boys could be out in the field when the men came to work.

Mama was up even before her husband and her sons. The wood stove was heated and ready to bake the turnovers that Mama rolled out and filled with apples before starting breakfast. Several loaves of bread and rolls were made the day before and were covered to keep fresh. Once the turnovers were out of the oven, Mama had two roast beef and a pork roast to cut up and cook by boiling them on the top of the wood-burning stove until they were tender. She thought about cooking a chicken or two to add to the meat available for the hungry men but knew the chickens would be needed for dinner. Jars of homemade pickles lined the counter. Apples and pears were in bushel baskets on the floor.

Mama counted the mason jars to make sure she would have enough for each man from which to drink. She would need to make coffee and tea to serve with lunch. Keeping the coffee warm on the wagon ride to the field was difficult. Chances are the tea and coffee would both end up warm instead of hot or cold. At least, it would be something other than water for the men to drink with their lunch.

Crocks of water were kept cool with burlap bags soaked in water and wrapped around the crocks. It was better than lugging out buckets of water for the men.

A hearty breakfast was next on her list to do. She would need all the loaves of bread to make sandwiches for the threshing crew, so she decided to serve dinner rolls with the ham, eggs, fried potatoes, and pancakes at breakfast. By 9:00 AM, Mama would need to take out food for the men who were working in the fields since 7:00 AM. That was a whole other meal to be prepared.

Mama's own hungry family, who were up since 4:00 AM to milk the cows, feed the animals, separate the milk and clean the separator, filed in for breakfast before the ham was completely fried. A stack of pancakes was piled high with butter and was on the table with jelly to spread. Abby came in, carrying the baby who woke when the door slammed as Daniel and William entered the house.

"Hand me the baby, Abby. I can hold him while I eat," Papa said, holding out his hands to take the squirming bundle.

"How is my little man?" chortled Papa as he bounced George up and down on his lap.

Abby, feeling a bit jealous of the attention Papa was giving the baby was about to make a peevish comment when Mama beckoned her to the stove.

"Abby, take the ham over to the table and sit down. I will bring the eggs and more pancakes in a moment."

A massive bowl of scrambled eggs was placed in the center of the table beside the platter of ham. The boys were already eating mouthfuls of pancakes with strawberry jam. Flipping the last pancakes on the griddle, Mama prepared herself to take the baby and feed him while her family finished their breakfast.

Folding a pancake in fourths, Mama ate it while she nursed the baby and talked to her husband about the possible timetables.

"Do you think the crew will come to our farm first? Do they usually let the farmer know before they arrive, or do they just show up?" Mama asked with some concern.

Papa answered with a question. "What did they do last year, Lenora? I don't remember."

"They just showed up.... It is challenging for us women to prepare food when we don't know if they are coming sooner or later," Mama complained.

"You are going to serve them the same thing either way, so it doesn't really matter, does it?" Papa said pragmatically.

Mama sighed. "I suppose you are right. We women just like to have some notice, that is all."

Mama was about to say how women are taken for granted it and how hard they worked on the farm when Papa spoke.

"I know it is not fair for our women. There is a whole lot of work on a normal day, and when one adds in work to feed an extra 20 men for two days, that is asking an awful lot. No city woman could do what you do. I am grateful you accepted my proposal. I can't imagine what life would be like without you."

Hearing her husband say such complimentary words made Lenora's heart melt. Knowing her husband appreciated all her efforts made the work seem less painful. Lenora told herself she was lucky to have a man who truly appreciated her.

"I am pretty fortunate to have good neighbors. I don't think I could get lunch out to all of the crew without the help of Mrs. Granger and Mrs. Mueller. I can repay Mrs. Mueller when it is time for the threshing crew to come to her house, but Mrs. Granger doesn't farm anymore now that her husband is deceased. I will need to think of some special way to thank her. She is such a dear woman," Mama said.

"Boys, if you have eaten your fill, we need to get the small wagon hitched to old Saul and have him brought under the tree so Mama can bring the lunch out. I don't want Mama to have to hitch up the wagon. Old Saul will be fine if you make sure he has his feed bag to keep him occupied," Papa told the boys. "Lenora, you will need to unhitch him and put him in the corral so he can get water after you come home."

Daniel said, "That is a long time for Old Saul to have to just stand in place, don't you think, Papa. How about if William comes home a little before lunch and hitches him to the wagon. William is going to need a break by then anyway."

Papa looked at his oldest son. "You know, Daniel. I think you are right. Old Saul would get awfully stiff, just standing in one place for hours. That is a good suggestion for William to leave before lunch to hitch the old horse to the wagon. It will also be a good way for your mama to know we are ready for lunch."

William didn't complain. He was glad to be able to get out of some of the hard work of loading sheaves of wheat into the threshing machine. By lunchtime, William knew his body would be aching in every muscle imaginable. He appreciated the fact that Daniel knew he was not as strong as himself and that Daniel was protecting him. He decided he would need to do something nice for Daniel, but he wasn't sure what just yet.

Mama completely missed the fact that Papa and Daniel were trying to protect William from working so hard. She said, "Don't be silly. I can hitch the wagon myself. The other ladies will watch Abby and George while I do that. No sense in sending William home for something I can do in five minutes."

Papa shrugged, "Okay, if that is what you want."

As Papa and the boys left the house to go to the field, Mama looked at the pile of dishes that needed to be done before her helpers arrived. She did not want the ladies to think she was a messy housekeeper. Giving George to Abby, she went about stacking the dishes near the sink. Papa brought in wood and water before he went to the barn first thing in the morning. Heating two large pans of water to act as wash water and rinse water, Mama prepared to wash and dry the dishes. Wishing the baby would fall back to sleep so Abby could help, was a wasted wish. Baby George would be awake for hours before he would be ready for a nap.

Mama was just grateful George was a happy baby, and Abby was a good babysitter.

The dishes were barely dried and put away when Mama heard Mrs. Granger's buggy arriving. Shep, who usually gave warning of any approaching people was quiet. Mama knew that meant that Shep followed the team out to the field and was not in the front yard. There were plenty of rabbits for him to chase in the fields, but he would return when the threshing crew arrived with the noisy steam machine belching out black smoke.

Stepping out on the porch, Mama smiled and welcomed Mrs. Granger into the house. Mama walked out to show Mrs. Granger where she could get water for her horse. She indicated the shade tree would be a good place for the horse to stand to keep it cool during the heat of the day.

Mrs. Mueller would be dropped off by her husband when he came to help in the field. His wagon would be used to take some of the wheat to market. Mrs. Granger volunteered to take Mrs. Mueller home after lunch was served.

Mrs. Granger, always good-natured, went straight into the parlor to take the baby from Abby. Abby was glad of a break and went to her room to play with her doll.

"My, my, my... isn't George getting big? Pattycake, pattycake, baker's man," Mrs. Granger chanted as she brought George's tiny little hands together to make them clap.

Mama smiled and went back to the kitchen. "Can I get you a cup of coffee or tea, Mrs. Granger?" Mama hollered from the other room.

"No, thank you, Lenora," Mrs. Granger remarked. "I took tea with my breakfast. I just want to play with the baby for a few minutes before Mrs. Mueller comes and takes him away from me."

The ladies chatted back and forth from the two separate rooms. Mama cut loaves of bread into slices in preparation of making forty sandwiches grateful that Mrs. Granger was giving Abby a break.

It wasn't long before Mrs. Mueller was opening the door and rushing to take the baby from Mrs. Granger.

"See, I told you I needed to get here first, or I wouldn't get any time with the baby, didn't I?" Mrs. Granger laughed. "Good timing since the baby needs to be changed."

Mrs. Mueller wrinkled up her nose. "Phew! You are right. This baby needs his nappy changed badly. Are his diapers in your bedroom, Lenora?"

"You don't need to change him. I can come and do the dirty work," Mama said, wiping her hands on her apron.

"No, I want to change him. It has been a very long time since any of my children were in diapers. It will be good training for me since Leland and Bertha are going to have their first child in two months," answered Mrs. Mueller.

The 9:00 AM breakfast was picked up by William and Daniel earlier to take to the crew. Mama prepared the threshing crew's breakfast at the same time that she made the family breakfast. Now the work for lunch was beginning.

The ladies chatted back and forth all morning as they prepared the lunch. Abby took over the chore of babysitting while the three women worked happily in the kitchen. The roasts were cooled and cut into thick slices. The chicken was cut and fried. Potatoes were also cut and prepared where the men could eat them with their fingers. The fruit was carried to the porch to be placed on the wagon once Mama hitched up Old Saul. Lots of water was heated for pots of coffee and tea. The turnovers were in baskets and ready to be taken out. It seemed everything was in order.

Mama excused herself to go and get the horse and wagon ready. The two women placed the bushel baskets of fruit into the bed of the wagon when Mama returned. Mrs. Granger rushed to her own wagon to retrieve the cookies she baked the day before to add to the food already prepared. Many trips were made by all, carrying food and drink, mason jars, and buckets of water for the men to use to wash up and towels to dry their hands. Dish pans lined with towels were used to carry the food to the men since there were no picnic baskets available.

Mama stopped and thought whether everything was on the wagon that was needed when she remembered her promise to Abby. "Mrs. Granger, would you and Mrs. Mueller be willing to stay and babysit George so Abby can see how the threshing machine works. I did promise her."

"It would be my pleasure to stay with this adorable little fellow. You take Abby, and George will be just fine here," Mrs. Granger said as she picked up the baby from the blanket on the floor where he had been kicking his chubby little legs in the air.

Abby danced, merrily all the way to the wagon until she saw Old Saul and couldn't resist walking under his belly and between his legs. "Abby Dolen, you get out from under that horse's belly. Do you want to be kicked in the face?" Mama scolded.

"Old Saul would never kick me. I always walk under his belly. He thinks it is a fun game, don't you, old boy?" Abby said while smiling out from under the old horse's front legs.

"Now, Abby! I don't want you to crawl under the horses ever again. It is just too dangerous. You never know when a horse will spook, and then you would be trampled. Promise me you won't do this again!" Mama said with her stern, no-nonsense voice.

Abby crawled out from under the horse. She went to the wagon, where Mama lifted her up on the seat. They traveled to the field in silence. Mama probably thinking about all the horrible things that could have happened to her little girl. Abby knew better than to draw attention to herself while Mama was still upset.

The threshing crew cheered when they saw the wagon drawing near. The men were hungry and thirsty from a hard morning's work. Mama knew the men would devour the food in minutes without hardly tasting one bite until their stomachs were full. Already Mama's mind was on preparing a late afternoon snack for the men before they retired for the day. All the hard work would start over again in the morning before the crew would go on to the next farm. That meant Mama would have another hard day. Thankfully, the two women promised to return the next day to help with the final preparations. Mama would return the favor and be at Mrs. Mueller's house when the crew ended up there.

Harvesting was not going to be complete once the crew left. The corn would need to be shelled, the hay baled, and food from the garden and orchard would need to be preserved for the long winter months when nothing could grow under the snow.

Unpacking the food and mason jars filled with tea or coffee, the men gathered to see what was on the menu. Excited voices raised louder at seeing the turnovers and cookies. Mama thought to herself that men never really grew up. They were still little boys when it came to having dessert.

As the men finished their lunch and sat in the shade of the wagons for a few minutes before returning to the hot work, Papa came to Mama's side and told her to take William home for a rest. "He just is too small to work all day. I would send Daniel home as well, but he is keeping up with the men. I need his help even though I feel bad that he is doing a grown man's work when he is just a boy."

Mama looked at Daniel. He stood taller than most of the men in the field. His body was streaked from dust turned to mud from his sweat. He laughed with the men and seemed to fit in.

William sat exhausted against one of the wagon wheels. There was no smile or joking with the crew. Mama felt sorry for her son. She knew he worked just as hard as Daniel without the results. He would never be as strong as his older brother, but he would try doubly hard to keep up with him. Mama knew William would protest when Papa told him to go home with his mother and little sister. Mama knew she would need to find a way for him to save face.

Gathering the last of the dishpans and boxes of mason jars, Mama shouted to William, "William, the pump on the windmill is broken. I need you to come home with me now and fix it. You have a mechanical mind. I know you can figure out what is wrong with it. I can't wait for your father to come home. You can return to the field later."

William jumped to his feet, suddenly rejuvenated. "Yes, Mama. I will get the tools to fix it as soon as we get home."

Mama felt saddened that Daniel would realize the whole thing was a ruse when they got home and found the windmill pumping fine. At least, he saved face in front of all the men. She could deal with her deception when they got home.

CHAPTER THIRTEEN

The hard work and festivities of harvest were over for another year. Thanksgiving was just around the corner, and the children had been back in school for over a month. Abby, precocious as ever, demanded to start kindergarten even though she would be the youngest child in the school. Miss Turnbull accepted her as a student after sitting down and discovering she already knew her alphabet, could count to one hundred, and was able to write her own name. Proudly, she told Miss Turnbull that William taught her everything.

Mama missed her babysitter. Now, Mama needed to do all her chores with one eye on George or hauling him around on her hip. The baby was growing quickly, and he was into everything. Mama almost thought of telling Abby she must stay home one more year, but the excitement on her face erased that idea from Mama's mind. She could not dampen her daughter's desire to learn.

Mama completed the eighth grade, but never got a chance to go any further in school. In her day, women were not expected to be educated. Helping their mothers and learning the necessities of keeping a home was considered a girl's education. Mama secretly wished she would have been able to go to high school and graduate. Mama would make sure her daughter got the opportunities that she never had.

Mama was grateful that she knew how to cook, clean, sew, can, and grow fruits and vegetables. Her mama taught her well. Mama could read the Bible to her children, so her education was not wasted, but a part of her wanted more. Papa said once the children were grown and they could retire, that she could take night courses or whatever she wanted to do.

Right now, Mama needed to think about hosting the Thanksgiving dinner for the whole family. It was her year to have everyone out to the farm. Mama would supply the turkeys, and everyone else would bring dishes to share. It would be too cold for everyone to eat outside, so Papa arranged to rent the church's social hall for the day. Getting up early to cook the turkeys and trying to keep them warm to take to the hall was going to be difficult. Papa finally told her the turkeys did not need to be warm, just tasty. That took some of the strain off Mama's back.

The social hall possessed plenty of tables and chairs and a kitchen large enough for the women to work in without bumping into each other too often. The dishes were available for their use as long as everything was cleaned and returned to its rightful place, all would be well.

Aunt Gladys was in charge of thinking of games the children could play inside. Most likely, there would be snow on the ground. It so often happened that the first snow was on Thanksgiving. If that were the case, the families would bring sleds, and the children could play outside until they got too cold. Hot cocoa would be waiting for them as a special treat when they came inside before eating.

There were twenty-one children in all when the families gathered. Daniel was not the eldest of the grandchildren, but he was number two in order. Baby George was still the youngest even though Eloise, Mama's sister-in-law, was due within two months. Everyone was excited about the arrival of the newest member of the family. Until that time, George would be passed around from aunt to aunt.

When the day finally arrived with snow on the ground as predicted, Papa hitched the team to the family sleigh. There was just room for all of them. The two turkeys and the ham were strapped to the back of the sleigh in a covered compartment. Mama wanted to arrive first at the social hall to make sure the tables and chairs were set up according to her design. She would not make place cards to assign seating, but she thought it was best to keep Uncle Henrich away from Uncle Will, William's namesake. The two men had gotten into a fight ten years ago, and neither was willing to shake hands and makeup. Mama thought they were fools. However, she would try to make sure they kept their distance from each other so as not to ruin the family dinner.

The snowy air was crisp and cold, and the family huddled under blankets. Everyone was in good cheer. The children were excited to be able to play with their cousins. Papa was excited about all the excellent food. Mama was just happy to be able to see her sisters and brothers again. It had been several months since she had seen them all at one time.

William looked out over the back of the sleigh and watched the tracks being made in the snow. The two parallel lines usually straight occasionally swerved as the sleigh slid around the corners. Mama's voice rang out in the cold air, and she led her children in a song called "Over the River and Through the Woods." Even though the family was not going to Grandmother's house today, Grandma would be at the gathering.

Papa took care of the team as the rest of the family helped Mama carry in the food for the dinner once they arrived at the church. William carried George in but set him down immediately when they entered the social hall. Abby took charge of her baby brother once he was on the floor.

Mama's first order of business was to start the fire in the stoves. The church owned two large wood-burning stoves. Mama knew it would soon heat up the social hall, and some of her sisters and sisters-in-law would need to reheat their food before everyone sat down to eat together.

"Daniel, before you take off your coat, run out and see if Papa needs help with the team. William, I will need for you to help me in the kitchen until your aunts arrive." Mama shouted orders.

"Mama, that is women's work," William said with a twinkle in his eye, knowing it would get a rise out of his mother.

Looking irritated for only a moment, Mama saw that William was just teasing her, and laughed as she brushed back a lock of chestnut hair that escaped her tight bun. Handing Williams a stack of plates, she told him to start setting the table.

"Let's see," Mama said more to herself than William, "we should number thirty-four this year. Norman and his family are not going to be here. They are going to Sarah's family for the holidays."

"Darn! Daryl is my favorite cousin. Now I will only have girl cousins my age to play with. I hope they are willing to play outdoors. I want to build snow forts and have a snowball fight. Sometimes the girls don't want to play the same games I want to play." William complained.

Daniel walked in and overheard William's complaint. "Oh, come on! You know that Millie can out-throw any of us guys. She won't want to miss a snowball fight. Besides, why would you think you need to only play with the cousins the same age as you. We have always played as a large group."

Mama listened but stayed out of the conversation. She was busy gathering the eating utensils to be placed with each plate. "Daniel, help your brother finish setting the table. The family will be arriving soon, and I want as much done as possible since we are in charge of the Thanksgiving dinner this year."

Daniel didn't argue. He knew his mother was feeling a little stressed with having the responsibility of the dinner this year. She wanted everything to be just right. Mama made a centerpiece for the serving table the night before, and she was placing it on the long table reserved for food. She fidgeted with the greens and cranberries that brightened the decoration.

Laughter could be heard from outside as Papa greeted the first guests. Daniel and William both rushed out to see which relative arrived first, hoping it would be their favorite cousins so they could start to play. Abby was excited when Grandma entered with Aunt Louise. Abby knew Grandma would immediately take over the care of baby George and Abby would be free to play, too.

Giving Abby a big hug, Grandma set her coat down and went to the baby as Abby knew she would do. Mama poked her head out of the door to the kitchen and yelled across the large room.

"Hi, Mother, I see you have been put to work already. Louise, come on in the kitchen. The boys will carry in whatever you need from your sleigh."

Grandma picked up George and followed Louise into the kitchen. She could play with the newest grandson as she chatted with her daughters and daughters-in-law. Setting George on the floor, Grandma gave the baby two wooden spoons and a pot to entertain him. Over the loud noise, the baby made as he hit the pan with the spoons, Grandma told Mama that once the food was taken from Louise's sleigh, the men and Papa's team needed to go down the road.

She explained, "Uncle Will's automobile is stuck in the snow. He will need to have the team pull that darned contraption out of the ditch. I told Will that buying that machine was a mistake, but would he listen to me? No, of course not."

Louise laughed, "I forgot, Will was in the ditch. Meryl and Lyle will get him out in a jiffy. If we had room in the sleigh, we would have brought Eloise and the kids with us instead of leaving them by the side of the road."

Mama was horrified. "Is Eloise alright. After all, she is very pregnant. Did she hurt herself when the automobile slid off the road?"

"She said she was fine. The children were all giggling and making fun of their father's driving abilities. No, I would say everyone survived the mishaps," Grandmother offered.

Mama could hear Papa hollering for Daniel to come along. Daniel was as good with the team as Papa was, and he knew he may need some help if the horses got spooked by the automobile. Mama started to worry about the safety of her oldest boy. Imagining the worst was something Mama was known to do.

"Don't worry, Lenora," Grandma said comfortingly. "You married a good man. He won't let Daniel be in any danger."

Mama knew that to be true, but accidents happened, and when horses were involved, things could get out of hand quickly. Mama never really liked being around horses.

"I want to go watch the automobile getting pulled out of the ditch, too!" Abby announced.

"They don't need a little girl in the way, Abby. You stay here where it is safe and warm," Mama said.

"That is not fair. Why don't I get to do anything fun just because I am a girl? When I grow up, I am going to do dangerous things all the time to make up for not having any fun now!" Abby pouted.

Grandma laughed, and Abby became even madder. "I mean it! I am going to be a cowgirl or a policeman!" Leaving the kitchen, Abby stomped her feet loudly on the floor as she retreated.

"My, my, my...that little girl has your temper, Lenora. You are going to need to deal with her soon, or she will be out of control,"

Grandmother said lovingly. "I remember you stomping off just like that more than once."

"I did not stomp," Mama retorted.

"Oh yes, you did," Louise added quickly. "You were the Queen of Stomp. I remember one time you stomped so hard that you bruised your foot and you limped for a week."

Grandma and Louise both laughed long and hard, remembering Lenora's little temper tantrum. Mama just looked at each of them with little humor until she could not resist laughing at herself with her mother and sister. She could not deny that they were right.

More of the family arrived. Most were chuckling at Will's predicament. The women brought in their food, and the children stayed out in the snow to play. The men attended the animals, and once they were taken care of, they entered the hall to talk about the weather, last year's crops, and what next year might bring.

Soon, the chugging of the automobile could be heard, and everyone knew the team was successful in hauling the machine out of the ditch. The men were ready to give some good-natured razzing to Will when he entered. Laughter announced Will's arrival into the hall.

"Okay, laugh away, but I am not the one who needed to unhitch a team and make sure they were sheltered. I won't have to hitch up a team when it is time to go either. I will just go out and jump in my automobile and drive away," Will said over the laughter.

"That is until you are in a ditch again..." continued the teasing from Will's brothers and brothers-in-law.

Henrich came in with his family, and his voice boomed above the crowd. "Whose piece of junk is parked in front of the church?"

Will immediately bristled. Roland went to Will's side and placed a hand on his shoulder to calm him. Everyone knew the two brothers did not get along ever since the two farmed adjacent farms. One thing after another seemed to cause hard feelings. When Eloise told Will that she wanted to move into town and leave farming behind, Henrich took that as a personal insult since the two brothers depended on each other to keep their farms operating. Years later, Henrich needed to leave his farm and go to the town as well. He resented his brother and blamed him for his failure.

Hilda, Henrich's wife, went straight to the kitchen. She tried hard to stay out of the fight. Secretly, she was thrilled to be living in town and not to be working as hard as she worked on the farm.

Grandma quietly told Hilda when she came into the kitchen that she needed to let Henrich know how much she hated farming. Grandma didn't like her boys fighting and thought Hilda's confession might go a long way to stop the feud.

"If you told Henrich how much you hated being a farmer's wife, maybe he could let go of some of his resentments towards his brother. This feud has gone on way too long. I am tired of it. You could help to bring it to an end," Grandma said confidentially.

The rest of the women pretended to be busy and not to overhear what Grandmother was saying. Hilda just shrugged her shoulders. Being the daughter-in-law and not the daughter sometimes made Hilda resent the interference of her mother-in-law.

"Henrich is a proud man. He loved farming. His failure at doing something he loved so much is more of the problem than anything else. It is hard for a man to fail. He needs a scapegoat. I don't want to be one of the reasons he feels he failed. If I tell him I hated what he loved, I will be the next target, won't I?" Hilda said in her defense.

Lenora talked in an upbeat, cheerful way to distract the conversation away from her mother and sister-in-law. "My everything smells so good. I believe we will be ready to eat as soon as Marty and Eula arrive with their brood. I have a children's table set up for the younger children, except for baby George, of course.

He will sit on my lap to be fed. Is everyone about ready to serve? We probably should call the children in so they can get out of their snow clothes and be ready to eat."

Marty and Eula arrived as Mama was trying to defuse the tension in the kitchen. Eula came in carrying two baskets filled with her superior mince meat pies.

"Hi everyone," Eula said as she entered. "I see dinner is about to be served. Sorry, we were a little late. We had trouble finding enough coats that fit all the kids. I just didn't realize how much Raymond had grown. I needed to get one of Marty's old heavy coats. This first snow caught me unprepared. I guess that means a trip to town to buy a new jacket for Raymond tomorrow. The stores will be opened the day after Thanksgiving, won't they Eloise?

Eloise seemed to be the person who was the authority on town life for the family, even though Hilda lived there as well. Hilda found herself feeling like an outcast when the sisters got together. Lenora sensing Hilda's discomfort and resentment went to her side.

"Hilda, you know more about the stores than Eloise since she doesn't get out as much as you since being pregnant. Are there any stores open tomorrow?" Mama asked directly of Hilda.

"As far as I know, the stores won't be opened until Saturday. I believe most stores are taking both Thursday and Friday off. However, the General Store should be open. I saw Ellie, the storekeeper's daughter, yesterday, and she said her father only closes the store for Thanksgiving, Christmas, and Easter. He is even open on the 4th of July."

Eula seemed grateful for the news that she could get a coat tomorrow for her growing boy. Hilda seemed grateful to be included in the conversation, and Grandma had hopes that the women may be able to defuse the tension between her two sons.

The children came in tracking large amounts of clumped snow from the bottoms of their boots. Mama knew she would need to clean up the hall before leaving, so she quickly went to the door and told the children to take off their boots in one spot and not to track everywhere. As coats were piled on a back table, mothers started to dish up food for the younger children while their husbands got into lines to pile food on their plates. The women would be the last ones to serve themselves, making sure their husbands and children were settled before filling a plate.

At first, everyone was silent as they put food into their mouths. Before long, compliments were ringing out about how good everything tasted. The children were laughing and joking more than eating until parents would remind them to settle down and eat, or there would be no pie for them. With the threat of not having a dessert, the children's table quieted for a few minutes, but slowly the ruckus started again. Knowing it was a losing battle, the parents let it go.

With stomachs filled, gossip exchanged, and the social hall left as clean as it was found, each family gathered their exhausted children and headed for home, thankful for family time. The parents knew their children would fall asleep in the back of the sleighs, wagons, or in one case, an automobile.

On reaching home, Papa noticed Shep sitting in the open gateway of the barn lot. The gate was accidentally left unlatched. If not for Shep, all the cattle would have gotten loose. Papa exhaled low and slow with a whistle. Thank God for Shep. Not a single cow escaped. Papa realized what an asset the collie was and vowed to give him a large slice of left-over turkey.

CHAPTER FOURTEEN

Winter snow continued without a break for many days. Trudging through the snow to get to the barn was difficult for William, whose legs were much shorter than his taller brother's legs. Each step felt like ten. William's boots would sink a good foot down into the snow, and he would need to lift his foot up and over the mound for the next step. Falling often from being off-balance or stuck in the snow, William hollered for his older brother to slow down and help him.

Daniel barely heard William's voice over the howling wind. The flaps of his cap were pulled down over his ears, and a scarf covered the lower half of his face. William's muffled voice caught Daniel's attention, and he stopped and turned around. Wanting to laugh at the sight of his brother floundering in the snow where he had fallen, Daniel knew better than to do more than chuckle. William was furious with the efforts it was taking to get out of the deep snow.

"Give me your hand. I will pull you to your feet. Now is not the best time to be making snow angels," Daniel said with the grin that didn't hide the laughter in his voice.

"Ha-Ha, not funny!" William snarled under his breath. William, usually even-tempered when around his parents, littler siblings and classmates, found time spent with Daniel irritating. His older brother knew how to get under his skin and took every opportunity to do so.

"Come on. We have chores to do before we can get back to the house and eat some warm food. Thank goodness we don't have school today. I wouldn't want to have to walk all that way in the snow, and I doubt Papa would let us take Jack without a barn at the school to shelter him," Daniel said casually.

"I don't like snow!" William complained as he was dragged to his feet.

"You liked it just fine on Thanksgiving when we were sledding down the hill near the church. You seemed to enjoy it when you were sending snowballs into the faces of your cousins. I think you like snow just fine, except when you need to work in it," Daniel reasoned.

Once again, trudging along beside his bigger brother, William answered as he periodically grabbed Daniel for support to navigate a particularly deep drift of snow. "Snow can be fun, I guess."

Opening the barn door where the animals were housed all night brought multiple vocalizations from the beasts contained within. The horses nickered, expecting oats and hay while the cows softly mooed their greetings. The hogs that were not slaughtered for meat were in a special pen Papa made for the cold winter months. One old sow oinked and turned her cumbersome body to watch the boys in anticipation of her breakfast. Doves cooed from the rafters as the barn cats added to the chorus.

The barn smelled ripe. The animals each added their own unique odors. Despite the smell, the barn was warm. The heat given off by the animals made it cozy. Daniel took off his scarf and heavy coat, leaving his overalls and long-sleeved shirt as protection needed for any chill that may be in the air.

Climbing up the ladder to the hayloft, Daniel grabbed the pitchfork. He started shoveling massive amounts of hay down to the barn floor below where William gathered armfuls and carried them to the bellering, expectant gathering of cows. Soon all one could hear was the munching and chewing of contented animals.

"I will take care of the birds as long as I am up here," came Daniel's voice from the heights of the barn. William did not reply but continued the chores of feeding the various animals. Once the animals were all fed, milking the cows would take be the next duty on the chore list. The order of what was done each day did not change. That caused a peaceful mindset as the boys automatically did what was needed without thought or contemplation.

Daniel descended the ladder and took his spot on the three-legged milking stool at the left side of his cow to start milking while she continued to chew on the hay. The cats meowed and begged for fresh milk. Sitting up to catch the spray directed at them from an udder squeezed to produce milk, the boys laughed, even though this was an everyday occurrence.

"I am going to set some traps near the stream. Papa said he saw mink or weasel prints in the snow. We could sell the fur to the general store and get some extra money. Want to go with me?" Daniel asked?

"Not until the wind dies down. I don't plan to do anything that takes me out of the house until then," William answered.

Daniel just shrugged and continued to milk the cows. Before long, the chores in the barn were completed. The boys put on their coats, caps, and scarves for the return trip to the house by way of the spring house, where the milk would be separated at a later time. Daniel knew that Papa would ask them to do the chores to free up their mother since they did not need to rush off to school.

As they neared the house, Shep could be heard barking furiously, and the boys saw he had something pinned down next to the house.

"Probably just a raccoon," William said.

"Not unless it is rabid. You know raccoons aren't out in the daytime," Daniel answered.

"That is not totally true," William flung back at his brother, "raccoons are nocturnal, but we both know they get stuff done in the daytime as well."

Daniel knew his brother was right and didn't intentionally try to start a debate. At the moment, Daniel was too curious to see what Shep cornered. Getting within twenty feet of the farm dog, Daniel called Shep to his side so the cornered animal could be viewed. What Daniel saw immediately brought out his tender side.

"William, it is a small dog. He is half-starved and scared to death. He is shivering something awful. I am going to see if I can get him to come to me. You go in and let Mama know we have another mouth to feed," Daniel directed.

Daniel approached the quivering black and white terrier mix. Daniel could see he was young. Not being able to look at his teeth to see if his canine teeth were adult or still milk teeth made it difficult for Daniel to decide if the pup was over six months of age or older, but he knew he must be under a year. Directing Shep to sit and stay, Daniel knelt down and coaxed the scared dog to come to him.

"Come on, little fella. I won't hurt you." Pausing to see if the dog would relax at the sound of his voice, Daniel started up the conversation once again. "There is food in the house. Are you hungry?"

Daniel patted his leg and encouraged the young dog to come forward, but the little dog stayed with his short tail tight to his body, and his ears pinned back to his head.

The screen door could be heard to slam as Papa walked out to Daniel's side. Bending down, Papa picked the dog up into his arms and walked back to the house. Daniel stood in amazement, wondering why he had not thought to do the same thing in the first place.

Inside Abby and Mama were heard to be saying things like, "Poor little dog" and "how cute!" and the likes while Daniel struggled out of his coat, boots, scarf, and cap. Walking over to the kitchen, Daniel saw the terrier was already lapping up a bowl of oatmeal with bacon broken into pieces over the top.

Mama said while continuing to get breakfast on the table, "It looks like this little guy has not eaten for quite some time. I wonder where he came from and how far he has traveled."

"People drop off dogs in the country all the time. If they don't want them anymore, they figure they can fend for themselves out here. It is cruel. I once found a whole litter of puppies that someone dumped along the side of the road. Of course, they didn't make it," Papa said with a tinge of anger in his voice.

"We can keep this one, can't we, Mama?" Abby asked as she sat on the floor next to the little spotted dog.

"He won't eat much. I am sure he can stay here as long as Shep gets along with him. Sometimes animals get jealous of any new addition," Mama responded.

"Yay! I have a dog of my own," Abby sang in her annoying sing-song voice.

Papa immediately interjected, "He is not going to be a house pet if that is what you are thinking, young lady. This dog will have a job just like Shep. He will probably turn out to be a pretty good ratter. I hope he spends most of his time in the barn helping out those barn cats. I noticed more mice in the barn now that the snow is on the ground. I sure don't want them destroying our grain."

"Then, it is settled. We have another dog. What shall we call the pup?" Mama asked.

"Today is the Friday after Thanksgiving. Why don't we just call him Friday?" William suggested.

"Friday it is," Papa said with authority as the family sat down at the table to eat. Abby's eyes did not leave the young dog as he licked the bowl clean and settled down next to the stove for warmth.

"I think Friday is going to be my best friend," Abby added as she chewed a piece of bacon.

Shep immediately took to the new dog, Friday. It seemed the big dog enjoyed having another dog to play with when the children were at school or doing chores. The two dogs ran circles in the snow, and Friday curled up next to Shep for warmth when he was not in the barn.

At first, the barn cats took cover when Friday came into the barn. His frantic barking and constant erratic movements bothered the cats. Within days, the cats came out from their hiding places, knowing the dog was not going away. If they wanted milk treats, they knew they would need to brave the new strange animal.

One cat stood its ground as Friday came yapping close to its face. Snarling, hissing, and raising its fur to look twice its standard size caused Friday to hesitate momentarily. A strike from a front paw with claws extended, taught Friday to keep his distance from this formidable cat.

Friday proved to be a great ratter. The cats weren't always happy to have the small dog routing around the straw, jumping up on bales of hay or barking when he found a rat or mouse. More often than not, the cats scampered into hiding places to find peace when the annoying little dog was in the barn.

Daniel watched the small dog one morning as he jumped straight into the air and landed with stiff front feet onto a pile of snow. Repeatedly, the small dog did the same movement until a rabbit bolted from under the snow, and the chase was on. Zig-zagging across the field to escape the little dog, Daniel was fascinated to see Friday maneuver to stay on the rabbit's heels.

"William, watch Friday, go. He is staying on that rabbit, like crazy," Daniel said to his brother.

As the two boys watched, Shep came out of nowhere and pounced on the rabbit. The two dogs were working as a team, and Daniel immediately came up with an idea.

"William, let's go hunting," Daniel said as he turned to his brother. "Mama would love a change of menu. She said we could only hunt rabbits when there was snow on the ground so we wouldn't get rabbit fever. Well, there is snow on the ground, and it seems we will be able to catch at least a brace of rabbits without a gun. You know Mama hates for us to carry guns when Papa is not with us. What do you say? Are you up for some hunting?"

William, excited for something other than pork, beef, or chicken, called the dogs to his side. "Let's go. We don't have all day, you know."

The dogs seemed to understand that they were going to get to do something fun with the boys. Friday raced in circles around the boys as they walked out into the barren fields. Shep, wagging his tail, walked along behind the two boys, contented to be part of the team.

Before long, the race was on. Friday ferreted out another rabbit, and Shep was in pursuit. It seemed the dogs knew exactly what the boys wanted them to do.

"How does Friday find the rabbits so quickly?" William asked. "Sometimes I can see that the snow is a bit yellow when a rabbit is under the mound. I guess the yellow coloring is from the rabbit's breath, but dogs are color blind, so Friday doesn't see the yellow color of the snow."

"For a smart boy, you can sure act dumb. You know dogs can smell hundreds of times better than us, maybe even thousands of times better," Daniel said smugly.

"Yes, I did know that. I was just thinking about how much better our sight was than theirs when I asked about the yellow snow. Of course, I know dogs can smell more than we can," William said defensively.

Forgetting the conversation, the boys retrieved the rabbit from Shep and continued walking over the dried stalks poking out of the snow mounds where corn once grew. The day was young, so the boys were not content with two rabbits or a brace of them, as Papa would say. They continued walking behind the dogs for two hours, and within that time, the dogs were able to find four more rabbits to be cooked for dinner.

Mama would be happy to fry the rabbits for dinner once the boys cleaned them. With the new-found disease tularemia discovered only twenty years earlier, Mama was very cautious about ever handling dead rabbits any time of the year except winter. She worried about the cats and dogs getting sick from ratting all the time and made sure the boys alerted her if any of the farm animals acted ill. With the snow on the ground, Mama would be sure the rabbits would be disease-free; however, she would scrutinize the rabbits to make sure they were healthy before allowing the boys to clean them.

Returning home, the boys called excitedly to Mama to come out on the porch to see their catch. Wiping her hands on a towel, Mama poked her head out of the door but did not venture onto the porch where it was cold.

"My goodness! What have you boys brought me?" Mama said with a new-found excitement.

"Rabbits, Mama," William called out as he held up the two rabbits that he carried home. "Can we have them for dinner?"

"Hang on a minute while I put on a coat. It is cold outside, but I want to inspect the rabbits before you clean them for me." Mama said as she pulled on a heavy jacket hanging on a hook near the door.

Looking at the rabbits carefully, Mama pronounced the animals as edible. "You make sure and dispose of the skins where the dogs won't get to them and make sure you wash your hands several times with soap even though you have gloves on. I will want to wash your gloves, so put them in the mudroom where I can clean them really well. You both have mittens that you can wear to school tomorrow since your gloves won't be dry by the time to leave for school."

Looking at the coats the boys wore and knowing she would not be able to wash them, she told the boys to hang them in the mudroom when they were finished with chores. Mama would need to brush the coats off and hope she got rid of any residue from the rabbits. There was only so much she could do to keep her children safe, but she would always try her best.

After school, the next day, Daniel asked William to go to check the traps with him. The wind died down, so William agreed.

"If we get some fur-bearing animals, we can sell them and help with the medical bills," Daniel reminded William.

"Maybe if we catch a mink, we can make lots of money. I hear mink fur is very valuable," William declared.

Trudging through the snow was still tricky. It took longer than anticipated to get to the river where Daniel placed the traps a day or so ago. Looking for landmarks, Daniel announced that the first trap should be in the thicket next to a huge rock.

Walking to the area, Daniel was disappointed to see that the trap was sprung. Poking around with a stick, Daniel saw that an animal had been caught. All that was left was the animal's paw.

"Dad said that an animal would chew its own leg off to get out of a trap. That seems to be the case here," Daniel said, studying the paw.

"That is terrible," William cried. "How desperate the poor animal must have been to chew its own leg off. I don't want to trap anymore. It makes me feel sick. What if Shep or Friday came down here and got caught in one of these traps?"

Daniel knew his little brother was soft-hearted. "You are right, William. These traps are cruel. We won't use these types of traps ever again."

As Daniel dug the bar out of the ground that was holding the trap in place, William took the chewed limb and tossed it as far away as possible. Both boys went and gathered the other traps to take back to the barn and store away, never to be used again.

"We will just need to find another way to make some extra money," Daniel said.

William perked up. "Maybe I can sell one of my stories to the newspaper. Just think how proud Mama would be to see my story in print."

"That is a good idea, William. Why don't you write a story about how cruel these steel-jaw traps are so other people won't use them ever again?"

"I think I just might do that," William said with a smile crossing his lips. "I might just change the world to be a better place to live in."

"I believe you will, William," Daniel said as he patted his brother on his back.

CHAPTER FIFTEEN

Winter fun was something the boys looked forward to when they were allowed to go out in the freezing weather. The one sled the children received for Christmas the year before, was used extensively for sliding down the steepest hill in the field. Screams of excitement were heard as the boys picked up speed and plowed into a snowbank. Time and again, the boys were seen pulling the sled up the hill, just to slide back down in record time.

Finally, the cold got the best of them, and they dragged the sled back to the porch and went inside to warm up. Mother watched the boys from the window and knew they were heading home. Having two cups of hot cocoa waiting for them caused looks of joy to spread across their faces.

"Mama, you always know just want we need," Daniel said. "You are the best Mother in the whole world!"

William took his cup and nodded his head enthusiastically in agreement. Repeating his brother's words, he said, "The very best Mother in the world!"

Abby came out wearing all the winter clothing she could find in her closet. "Mama, I want to sled, too," she whined.

"Honey, your brothers just came in to get warm. I don't think they will be ready to go outside for some time. Why don't you take off your coat and mittens and have a cup of hot chocolate with your brothers? Maybe afterward, they will be willing to go out with you and pull you on the sled."

"Aw, Mama, do we really have to pull Abby around on the sled? Can't she just go out by herself and slide down the hill like we did? She isn't a baby anymore."

"No," Mother said, "Abby is too young to go sledding by herself. In fact, I don't want her going down the steep hill. You can take her to the smaller hill for sledding, or just pull her for a nice long ride on the sled. She will be just as happy with a ride."

"Mama, we aren't horses!" Daniel said indignantly.

"I know you are not a horse. I have eyes, you know. You are a big brother, though, and that is what big brothers do," Mother remarked. "Big brothers take good care of their little sisters."

Slowing down on drinking their cups of hot chocolate to stall needing to go out into the cold air and snow just to please their little sister was more than evident to Abby.

"Mama, the boys are drinking slower than before just so they won't have to go out with me. Make them drink fast."

"Abby, take off your coat and be patient. It is only fair to let your brothers warm up before going out again," Mother said. "If you want the boys to take you for a ride on the sled, you should ask them nicely and not make demands. Think how fortunate you are to have two big strong brothers to pull you around on the sled?"

Abby did not take off her coat. She sat in the chair across from her brothers and glowered at them. When Mother was preoccupied with the baby, Abby said lowly, "You better hurry, or I am going to tell Mother that you dumped me out of the sled on purpose. She will be really mad at you."

Both boys looked at each other, and a wicked smile crossed Daniel's face. Abby missed the exchange, or she might not have gone outside with them.

Once outside, William started pulling Abby around while Daniel disappeared into the barn. When he returned, he came out carrying a rigging that he put on Shep. He pulled the dog towards the sled and told William he could stop pulling Abby around. Shep would do the work.

Abby seemed excited about having her own sled dog. "Mush, Shep, mush!" the little girl called out excitedly.

At first, Shep balked about being tethered to the sled. He laid down in the snow and refused to move. Abby shouted louder for the dog to mush.

Daniel took hold of the rigging and pulled Shep to his feet. "Come on, lazy dog. Don't act like a goat. Let's run!"

Pulling and running, Shep finally decided it was a game. He pulled with all his strength and got the sled moving. As they approached a hill, Shep, scared when he found the sled was chasing him, ran zig-zagging away for the perceived monster nipping at his heels. Between the momentum of the hill and the dog's increased speed to escape the sled, Abby found herself in a neck-breaking race to the bottom where she found herself flung face-first into the snowbank. Unable to get to her feet, she flailed around with her arms and legs until her big brother lifted her to her feet.

Frozen, sparkling ice crystals clung to her face and clothing. "You look just like a snowman!" Daniel laughed.

Crying, she shouted, "I'm telling Mother on you. You did that deliberately. You just didn't want to play with me."

Running to the house, Daniel could hear her crying loudly and calling for her mama.

"Oh, oh! We are in big trouble now," Daniel said.

"What do you mean, 'we'? I was pulling her on the sled like Mama asked us to do. You were the one who rigged Shep to the sled. I think you are in trouble, not me."

"Great!" Daniel said. "I rigged up Shep so you would not need to pull Abby around. I did that for you, and now, you are going to leave me to take all the blame?"

"That is exactly what I am saying," William said. "I see Mama at the door, and she does not look happy. I think maybe you better go get your punishment out of the way while I untangle Shep."

Daniel trudged back towards the house, giving William one last look of betrayal. As he took off his boots in the mudroom, he could hear Abby retelling her story. It seems the first telling was not understood by Mama as Abby sobbed through it.

"Daniel, what do you have to say for yourself?" Mother said with her hands on her hips. "Didn't I tell you that a big brother's job is to take care of his little sister? It does not seem as if you listened to what I said. I think you should go to your room. When your father gets home, we will be having a family discussion."

"But Mama, I didn't do anything wrong," Daniel pleaded his case. "I just thought it would be easier for Shep to pull her than William or myself, and Abby loved it until she fell in the snow. How was I supposed to know that would happen?"

"Maybe some time in your room will help you discover that yourself. Now go!" Mother said furiously.

Abby stuck out her tongue at her brother as he passed her on the way to his room. Daniel thought that being sent to his bedroom wasn't such a bad punishment. He was tired, and a nap was just what he needed.

It wasn't until he heard the door slam, and he listened to his father greeting his mother that Daniel realized his punishment was yet to come. Putting his ear to the door, Daniel listened as Mother told his father what happened that day.

"Daniel!" Father's voice boomed, calling his son into the living room.

As Daniel came out from his room, he could see everyone seated except the baby, who was playing on the floor. He looked at his father's stern face and gulped.

"What do you have to say for yourself, young man?" Father asked, looking grouchy and irritated.

"I didn't mean for Abby to fall in the snow. I just thought that men use dogs to pull sleds all the time in Alaska and places like that. We have Shep, and he is a big strong dog, so why not harness him to the sled and let him do the work?"

"Dogs need special training to pull sleds. Shep has no training, and from what I understand from your brother, Shep became afraid when the sled came rushing down on his heels. You surely must have known that Shep would react that way. What were you thinking?"

"Father, I guess I thought Shep was smarter than what he is," Daniel said in the way of explaining his actions.

"And I thought you were smarter than that," Father said disappointedly. "Your punishment will be that you must pull Abby on the sled anytime that she asks for the next two weeks. You will pull her nicely and safely. Do you understand?"

"Yes, Father," Daniel answered meekly, not daring to look at Abby, who he knew would be smirking. "But what if she asks me to pull her when it is time for chores?"

"Abby will have her own chores at that time. She won't be asking you to pull her when she is doing her work," Father said and then dismissed the conversation. "In fact, it is time for your chores. Go outside and do them."

As Daniel pulled on his boots to go to the barn, William joined him. "I sure am glad that I did not come up with that harebrained idea to have Shep pull Abby around. I will enjoy my free time while you are pulling Abby."

"Ha, ha, ha," Daniel said. "At least, I will be getting bigger muscles, and you will stay a shrimp."

Daniel felt smug and self-satisfied that he was able to come up with a positive to his punishment. "I bet Ellie will notice my muscles."

The next morning, Abby was sick. She had a fever, sore throat, nausea, and a rash on her face and throat. Mama was not in the kitchen, making breakfast when the boys came in from milking the cows.

"Where is Mama?" William asked his father.

"I am afraid that Abby is sick. She won't be going to school. In fact, I am not sure that you boys will be going to school either. Mama thinks that Abby has Scarlet Fever. It is very contagious, and I am sure the doctor will quarantine our house. Mama called the doctor, and he said that I should come into town for medicine but not to come into the office or have contact with anyone. You boys are on your own for breakfast," Papa said as he pulled on his coat to go out to saddle Jack.

Daniel hung his head, "Is it my fault Abby is sick, Papa? I didn't mean for her to get covered in snow when I hitched Shep to the sled."

"No, Daniel, it is caused by a bacterium that she came into contact with when we were around someone who was sick," Papa said, trying to alleviate Daniel's sense of guilt. "You and William may have been exposed to the illness, too, so you won't be going to school until we know if you have been infected. We sure don't want to spread the disease around."

As Papa reached the door, he turned back with one more comment. "You and William are not to go upstairs at all. You two will be sleeping down here until Abby is well. Mama will need to change her clothes and wash up before she can come downstairs.

Mama is going to need a lot of help with George since we don't want him getting sick. That means double work for both of you."

"I guess we best make ourselves some breakfast," William said. "I will make the ham if you will make the eggs. Want me to holler up the stairs to see if we should make something for Abby?"

"Sure, holler up the stairs and see what Mama wants us to do about George, too. Maybe he can eat some scrambled eggs," Daniel said as he looked at his sleeping baby brother in the corner of his parent's room.

Mama said she was proud of her boys for thinking to feed their baby brother and told them she would be down soon after she went out the window to climb down the ladder to wash up and change clothes. Daniel looked worried that his mother was going to climb out of the window and down a ladder.

"Mama, I will hold the ladder when you are ready to climb down," Daniel yelled up the stairwell.

"That would be nice, but don't touch my clothes. I will need to burn them after Abby is well. In the meantime, my clothing will need to be kept away from everyone. I will wash up in the springhouse. I have a clean change of clothes already out there.

The next week was spent with Mama climbing up and down the ladder several times a day, washing herself and changing clothes after she attended her sick daughter. The boys never touched her contaminated clothing since Mama was adamant that they may not.

Baby George became fussy since he was not getting as much attention from his mother as usual. He also missed Abby, who was his primary source of entertainment. Everyone took turns holding him when Mama was with Abby, which seemed to be most of the time. Mama even slept upstairs so she would hear Abby if she started to vomit.

Before too long, what seemed like a century or two, if one asked the boys, Abby's skin started to peel as did her tongue, and the family knew she was on the mends. None of the rest of the family came down with any of the symptoms, so when Mama announced that it was time to burn her clothes, the family rejoiced and watched the bonfire burn any germs that might be left on the clothing and bedding.

William and Abby were ecstatic that they could return to school. Daniel, not so much.

CHAPTER SIXTEEN

Nothing stays the same. The children found out that Miss Turnbull resigned and was getting married when they returned from their Christmas break. Everyone was heartbroken, but especially Oscar, who secretly dreamed that someday he would marry the teacher. Until a replacement could be found, the students were to return to their homes

Home for Daniel and William had not been the same since their father passed away from a sudden bout of pneumonia, probably brought on by breathing the abundance of dust from the drought. Mama's brothers and uncles pitched in to help as much as they could; however, most of the duties fell to Daniel and William. The break from school was a blessing for Mama. Mama struggled with having the baby and Abby to care for as well as all her other chores. Leaving Abby to care for George while she helped the boys with chores left her feeling nervous and afraid for the baby. Mama knew Abby loved her little brother and would try her best to care for him for the short periods when Mama needed to be in the springhouse or out at the barn.

Money was a problem, so when Mama was approached about having the new teacher live with her, Mama accepted immediately. The extra income for renting out the room was a blessing.

Miss Finch was much different than Miss Turnbull. She was older and stern. Miss Finch did not feel that learning needed to be fun. She demanded that the children memorize most everything. Daniel, in particular, hated to need to learn poems by heart.

"Why do I need to learn poems, Mama? They are stupid. Listen to what I am supposed to know by heart

> *Snow falling and night falling fast, oh fast*
> *In a field, I looked into going past*

"That makes no sense, and it goes on and on and on," Daniel complained.

"Oh, that is Robert Frost's 'Desert Places.' It is beautiful, Daniel. You should learn it by heart," Mama said sadly "It reminds me of your papa."

William entered dramatically, holding his hands to his chest with his head tilted up to the ceiling and continued the poem without looking at the book.

> *And the ground almost covered smooth in snow,*
> *But a few weeds and stubble showing last.*

"I really like Emily Dickinson's poem better. It is more fun. Listen, Mama, I have already memorized it," William continued.

A Bird Came Down the Walk, by Emily Dickinson

> *A Bird came down the Walk*
> *He did not know I saw*
> *He bit an angle-worm in halves*
> *And ate the fellow, raw,*
> *And then he drank a Dew*
> *From a convenient Grass,*
> *And then hopped sidewise to the Wall*
> *To let a Beetle pass*

"That is enough!" shouted Daniel. "That just proves what I was saying. If William likes the poem, then, of course, it is stupid!"

Daniel slammed the porch door as he rushed out of the house.

"Well, that was rude," William said.

"William, your brother, does not have your gift for schoolwork. He finds memorizing very difficult. Maybe you could help him so that he does not get a bad grade. What do you say?"

"Mama, there is nothing I can do to help Daniel. He is hopeless. If he does not see the reason to do something, he just isn't going to do it. In fact, if I try to help him, he will probably hold me down on the ground and wallop me," William explained.

"I understand, William," Mama said. "I guess you best let me try to help him. Run along and get your chores done. Miss Finch will be moving in today, and I need to have dinner on the table when she arrives."

Mama was busy all day cleaning the room where Miss Finch would be staying. It was William and Daniel's bedroom, so making it more feminine was a chore that Mama happily accepted. The boys were moved into Abby's smaller room on the same floor. Abby would be sleeping with Mama and baby George.

When Mama heard the wagon coming down the lane, she gave the living room a once-over glance to make sure it was presentable and went to the porch to greet their new boarder. When the wagon pulled up in front, Mama was glad to see that Daniel and William were in the yard to help carry in Miss Finch's trunks.

"Welcome, Miss Finch. Come on in. The boys will bring in your trunks," Mama called out pleasantly

"Be careful with those trunks, boys. My most precious items are inside, and I would not want anything broken," Miss Finch said as her way of a greeting.

When Miss Finch stepped inside, Daniel grumbled sarcastically to William. "This is going to be fun. I don't think I am going to like having our new teacher living here with us. I have a feeling she will feel it is her place to tell us what to do all the time."

"Mama says we need the money, so I guess we are going to just have to put up with her in the house. I suggest you be on your best behavior if you don't want a scolding from Mama," William whispered.

Dinner was quieter than usual. Even Abby felt restrained from her general chatter. After all, Miss Finch was her teacher, too, and she wanted to impress her.

"Your children are very well behaved, Lenora," Miss Finch remarked.

"Thank you, Miss Finch. My husband made sure the boys were taught to be respectful. I hope they will mind their *Ps* and *Qs* in your classroom. I am quite sure that you are capable of handling rowdy boys when they do misbehave."

Looking sternly at Daniel, Miss Finch said, "I do have my ways with rowdy boys."

Daniel looked down at his plate and finished his last bite of food. Remembering to chew and swallow, he asked if he could be excused to bed down the animals. Mama nodded, and Daniel removed his plate from the table and put on his coat to go outside.

"I guess I had best help, Daniel," William said as he took his cue from his brother to leave and get out of doing dishes.

"I guess I had better help," Miss Finch said, correcting William.

"Oh no, Miss Finch. You stay. You don't need to come outside and help. I can do it," William said, totally missing the fact he had just had his language corrected.

Mama only smiled and turned her attention to Miss Finch to engage her in small talk to allow her second child to leave the house without more discussion on grammar.

Weeks turned into months with Miss Finch living in the house. Daniel found any excuse to be outside and away from the constant corrections Miss Finch seemed to think was her duty to inflict on him. William, however, seemed to thrive with having the teacher to impress. Abby, too, enjoyed the extra attention and praise she received for being such a smart little girl.

"Lenora," Miss Finch said one evening when the children were in bed. "Your two children are so smart. What happened to Daniel? He just does not apply himself like the other two do."

Mama stiffened. "Daniel is exceptional in other ways. He is the hardest working boy of his age that you will find anywhere. I can depend on him completely to do a man's job now that his father has passed away. I don't think you understand how difficult it is for an eleven-year-old boy to need to take on a man's work. I could not stay in my home if it were not for Daniel."

Miss Finch said nothing in reply. Instead, she resumed reading her book, but Mama noticed that she seemed to squirm a bit in her seat. Looking up from her book a few minutes later, Miss Finch said, "I understand your dilemma. You are in a hard place without your husband. I guess you are fortunate to have such a strong young son to help you out."

Mama smiled and thanked Miss Finch for her kindness. Mama thought that maybe Miss Finch was softening her attitude towards Daniel a bit until the next little episode.

It seemed the boys became aware that Miss Finch needed to use the chamber pot at the same time each night. The chamber pot was placed on the landing at the top of the stairs. That way, no one needed to go outside to the privy during the cold months.

Daniel, always ornery, talked William into playing a prank on Miss Finch. "Let's tie a string on the handle of the chamber pot, and when Miss Finch uses it tonight, let's pull it out from under her."

Laughing, Daniel thought the prank was hilarious until Miss Finch let out a scream as the chamber pot moved out from under her squatting bottom. Mama, hearing the screaming, came running out from her room and raced up the stairs where she found Miss Finch scolding the boys, shaking her index fingers in their faces while blustering out words of threats.

When Mama found out what the boys just did, she was beyond humiliation. "Clean up that mess right this minute and then meet me downstairs. Is that understood?"

"It was Daniel's idea, Mama!" William said with his eyes wide open and showing fear of his mother's anger.

"I don't care whose idea it was. You are both in more trouble than you can imagine!" Mama said as she followed Miss Finch into her room to apologize empathically.

Once the door was closed and the boys could not hear, Miss Finch smiled and patted Mama's hand. "I needed to be stern with the boys, but I have to admit that their little joke was rather funny in a crass way. It is something my brothers would have done as well. I told you that I know how to deal with ornery boys. I lived with four brothers, and each was ornerier than the other. I will let you handle this, but I believe that the boys will owe me a few favors at school for a week or two as well."

"I agree," Mama said. "That was bad behavior, and if their father was still alive, I know he would have taken them behind the woodshed for a spanking they would not have forgotten."

"I don't believe in spanking, but you know what is best for your own children. I will leave their punishment up to you," Miss Finch said, still chuckling.

William and Daniel got off easy with several extra chores around the house and two weeks of cleaning the chalkboards and losing recess at school. Both boys said to each other than the punishment was harsh. Each admitted to themselves that they had gotten off easier than if Papa were still alive. However, a spanking would have lasted for a minute or two, and then it would have been over. This punishment was lasting entirely too long.

The routine, since Miss Finch was in the house, included harnessing the horses to take Miss Finch to school each morning. Along the way, Daniel stopped to pick up several children. Usually, that meant that there was a total of seven people on the wagon each morning. The children would quietly talk amongst themselves on the bed of the wagon while Daniel drove the team, and Miss Finch sat upfront with him.

It was a lovely early spring morning, and meadowlarks were singing their pretty song as the team clip-clopped down the hilly dirt road. Papa had always told Daniel to stay on his side of the road while going uphill since one could not see if anything was coming from the other side. Daniel, lax from driving the team the same route every morning, allowed the team to pick their own path, knowing that the ruts in the road made it difficult for the team to stay on the right side. The middle was smoother and less difficult for Maud and Molly to navigate.

Everything seemed as if it was going to be a perfect day until one of those noisy gawdawful vehicles made a sudden appearance at the top of the hill, clunking and rattling so loud that Maud and Molly spooked and headed off the road in a panic. Hitting the deep ditch and racing through the field, children were deposited on the ground, scattered in all directions while Miss Finch and Daniel held on for dear life. As the wagon turned over, Miss Finch and Daniel also landed unceremoniously onto the ground as well.

The driver of the vehicle stopped to aid in the disaster before him. When he saw the children, all getting to their feet with nothing more than a few scrapes and bruises, the man hurried on towards Miss Finch, who was holding her arm carefully in her other hand.

"I fear you have a broken arm, Mam," the owner of the automobile said kindly. "Can I take you to the hospital?"

Looking around, Miss Finch said, "How are the children? Was anyone hurt?"

Daniel, racing after the team, seemed as if he was alright. The rest of the children assembled in front of Miss Finch for her inspection.

"It seems that the children are fine. I think you are the only one who got hurt. Please, let me take you to town."

Daniel leading the team back to the buckboard wagon. He asked if the man might help him and the children to right the wagon before the man took Miss Finch to the hospital. With a great effort from everyone, except Miss Finch, the wagon was set back on its wheels, and the team was hitched.

"Daniel, take the children home and then come and fetch me at the hospital," Miss Finch instructed.

"I will bring you back home. Daniel doesn't need to come to town. I think you will be more comfortable in my automobile than on the wagon," the kind stranger said.

"If it isn't a bother, then I accept your kind offer," Miss Finch said with a sweet smile.

Watching the man hovering to assist Miss Finch to the automobile, William was heard saying, "I think we are going to be in the market for another teacher."

Daniel was the hero. There was no school for two weeks while Miss Finch recuperated. William was right about his prediction. Miss Finch and the owner of the automobile did marry, and the school board looked for a new teacher.

Mama was saddened to lose the extra money. Abby was unhappy that she needed to return to her own room. Daniel was happy that he did not need to learn the poem to recite in front of everyone at the school program that was canceled. William was frustrated that he was not going to be able to show off that he knew more poems than anyone else, so he went around the house, spouting poetry until Daniel hit him.

CHAPTER SEVENTEEN

Boys don't remain boys forever, so Daniel and William grew to be good respectable men. They looked back and realized how difficult life was growing up on a farm during the great depression. They also looked back on their younger years with a sense of joy. They had food, family, and friends. They worked hard, and they played hard.

When news broke out about the war to stop dictators from taking over the world, both young men knew they needed to do their patriotic duty and join the service. Daniel joined the Navy, and William joined the Air Force.

Both survived the war with stories to tell, some funny, but most were sad. Losing friends was hard. Being shot down behind enemy lines was terrifying for William. Watching the point ship in the formation being sunk by a mine was also terrifying for Daniel. It was especially terrifying when his ship took the point position. Both young men came home wiser, stronger but no longer naive.

Ellie remained single, and Daniel found she was still smitten with him, and they were married. William, too, found a cute lady waiting for him. Both remained married to their special sweethearts for the rest of their lives.

The unions were blessed with a total of five children—three for Daniel and two for William. The men worked hard to provide support for these children and passed on the stories of their own childhoods. Being one of the children, I needed to tell some of those stories for others to enjoy. Of course, I changed the names of the characters to protect the innocent, as is often said. The delight I felt when hearing my father tell his stories has stayed in my heart, and I wanted to pass some of them on to the readers.

Both men are no longer on this earth, and neither are the lovely women they married. They are missed greatly by their children and grandchildren. Hopefully, their stories will allow other people to know these men as young boys as I have and love them as I do.

Carole Walker Carter

Starting life in a small town in Nebraska, Carole and her family moved from the Mid-West to the West Coast. Carole continued traveling from California to Texas, Ohio, back to Nebraska and finally settling in the Pacific Northwest with her husband, Don, her childhood sweetheart and partner, their dogs, and a few fish.

Carole's career involved working with children from pre-school through high school, dealing with special needs, and "at-risk'" children as an Occupational Therapy Assistant and Educational Assistant.

Meeting unique people throughout her life, fascinating characters formed in Carole's mind. These individuals shaped the basis for real and imagined characters found in her various forms of storytelling from Science Fiction, Detective, to her Children's Books.

Find her books on Amazon, Kindle, Nook, Apple Books, and Barnes & Noble Now by searching for *Carole Walker Carter*!

Aztara, The Mastel Kingdom
By
Carole Walker Carter

Aztara, The Mastel Kingdom, tells the background story of the majestic mastel creatures that roamed the rugged mountains and the fertile valleys of Aztara. The setting for this book is two generations before the plague that killed all the Aztarian women during Volume I, *Surtees, Science Rules*.

Idyllic as the lush lavender summer pastures might seem, the mastels are forced to be nomadic, dependent upon the weather and growing cycles for their diet. Equipped with spiraling horns and clawed feet, the stallions are always at the ready to protect the herd against terrifying river monsters and voracious tree-dwelling beasts.

The newly established bond between the cave-dwelling griswells and the mastels seems destined to fail, until Morsian, an inventor from the eastern factory villages, creates a symbiotic relationship that will change everything on Aztara…forever.

Explore the early world of Aztara and enjoy the Mastel's unique story.

Find this book on Amazon, Kindle, Nook, and Barnes & Noble Now!

Surtees, Science Rules
By
Carole Walker Carter

Surtees, Science Rules, is Volume I in the *Aztarian Series.*

In *Surtees, Science Rules,* we discover how ruthless a dystopian society can be when the ruler is a despotic scientist determined to achieve longevity to remain in power forever.

Ananaya brutally seizes power from his father, Ryndor, who set up several senior scientists as the leaders of scientific research centers. Under fear from retaliation, the scientists carry out the plans of Ananaya, which in turn, causes destruction to the air, water, and food supplies for the citizens of Surtees. As the Surtarians' lives crumble under the oppressive rule of Ananaya, two unlikely young females, Tawtanya and Myana, rise from champions of the Surtees Zrymir Games to become heroes of the planet.

Find this book on Amazon, Kindle, Nook, and Barnes & Noble Now!

AZTARA, A Galactic Love Story
By
Carole Walker Carter

AZTARA, A Galactic Love Story, Volume II in the *Aztarian Series*, centers on two main characters from two different planets whose lives are turned upside down by the ruthless scientist, Ananaya.

Shayla, an Earth woman, grieving for the loss of her only child and deceived and abandoned by his father, is close to suicide. A unique bond with fantastical creatures on her new home of Aztara helps Shayla to return to a balanced life in a strange new world.

Ty, having lived through a plague killing all the females on Aztara, finds refuge in his work, mining the mineral, phyrium, instrumental to all aspects of life on Aztara, including telepathy, longevity, and levitation.

Ananaya, the Chief Scientist from Surtees, leaves a dying planet to relocate on Aztara to seize control of the mineral phyrium for his own benefit. In his attempt to rebuild his army of Enforcers, he abducts Earth women who carry a specific gene, the warrior gene, to mate with the Aztarian men. This momentous event brings our two main characters together to face the seemingly insurmountable challenges of an intergalactic romance.

The story is about finding internal strength, trust, and love. Intrigue and thrilling moments prevail while the two main characters come to grips with a situation, not of their own choosing.

Find this book on Amazon, Kindle, Nook, and Barnes & Noble Now!

AZTARA, Secrets Revealed
By
Carole Walker Carter

AZTARA, Secrets Revealed, Volume III in the *Aztarian Series*, is the culmination of Ananaya's ultimate plan. The offspring of the intergalactic mating produce some surprises for the peaceful Aztarian men. Shayla's and Ty's love produced twins.

Nayela is the only interspecies girl on Aztara that bonds telepathically with a mastel. Kestle, jealous of his sister's abilities, has his hands full with being a gang member.

A tragic event occurs, changing everything for Kestle. Self-banished to the Wildlands leaves Kestle alone to deal with situations for which he was unprepared. Going deeper into the Wildlands brings Kestle to the dreaded Orange River, where dangerous monsters lurk. Saving a young runaway girl, Sinaka, from certain death. He discovers, however, there is more to this young girl than he first thought.

Sinaka finds it is her turn to save Kestle when a monster wounds him. With unexpected help from a beautiful creature and Sinaka's psychic and empathic powers, Kestle finds healing.

The Surtarian Chief Scientist, Ananaya, accelerates his plan to genetically modify the Aztarian/Earthling boys' Warrior Genes. Ananaya's plot is to create a daunting army of new Enforcers. All hell breaks loose when the usually passive Aztarians decide to fight to get their boys back.

Find this book on Amazon, Kindle, Nook, and Barnes & Noble Now!

Final Alumni
By
Carole Walker Carter

The Final Alumni is Volume I in the *Evers and McFarlan Detective Series.* This series follows two high school best friends who join forces to start careers as private investigators. Tish, haunted by a childhood experience, enables herself mastering many disciplines of martial arts, while Scotty falls back on his expert firearms training and physical prowess as a football quarterback.

Out of high school, the two go to Chicago, Illinois, to pursue their career through education and on-the-job training. Mentored by a well-respected couple who owns The Jamieson Detective Agency, Tish and Scotty are enlisted to assist Aileen and Patrick Jamieson in solving cases in Chicago while pursuing a series of unsolved murders in their own hometown as well.

Find this book on Amazon, Kindle, Nook, and Barnes & Noble Now!

Shadowy Faces
By
Carole Walker Carter

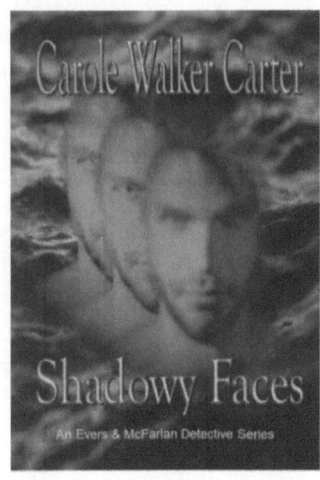

Shadowy Faces is Volume II in *the Evers and McFarlan Detective Series.* In *Shadowy Faces,* Tish and Scotty are confronted with the lives of three young women who have been ruined. Each young woman deals with lost weekends where all they can recall are vague faces tormenting them. The shadowy faces become the focus of the investigative team of Evers and McFarlan along with the Jamiesons and the Chicago Police department. The team works methodically to discover what happened to each of the women to bring the criminals to justice.

Tish needed to lean on a secret discipline her Grand-Master taught her even with the warning of what could happen to her if anyone should learn of her new martial arts fighting technique. Scotty also faces the threat of losing the love of his life

Find this book on Amazon, Kindle, Nook, and Barnes & Noble Now!

Nine Points of a Circle
By
Carole Walker Carter

Carole Walker Carter

Nine Points of a Circle

Evers and McFarlan Detective Series

Nine Points of a Circle is Volume III in the *Evers & McFarlan Detective Series*. In *Nine Points of a Circle*, Tish and Scotty are fully licensed detectives in The Jamieson Detective Agency. Even though the Jamiesons' are preparing to retire, they continue to mentor, advise, and direct Scotty and Tish on new cases.

Captain Jones tries to block Tish and Scotty from getting involved in what appears to be an intelligent yet spine-chilling serial killer. Three homeless girls were murdered over the past five days, and their bodies were dumped on different streets in greater Chicago. At the same time, Tish and Scotty are assigned to a serial robbery case and are approached by a well-known Chicago business executive regarding his missing daughter.

All three of the cases challenge Scotty's mathematical and technical expertise and Tish's detective and martial arts skills to solve. Follow Tish, Scotty, and Duma, their tracking canine, as they plunge themselves into the plight of the homeless on the dark and perilous Chicago night streets.

Find this book on Amazon, Kindle, Nook, and Barnes & Noble Now!

The Child Rowanda, Little Dragon
By
Carole Walker Carter

The Child Rowanda, Little Dragon Volume I, Twelve-year-old Rowanda lives with her mother and grandmother, an elder sorceress, in the lush garden planet of Neslora. Seemingly an idyllic world with endlessly blooming flowers, buzzing bees, and birds chirping...until.

A tyrannical king's guards abducted and transport several women of Neslora to the desert world of Arolsen, where they are being kept as slaves.

Rowanda and her friends discover, with horror, the abduction of their mothers. Armed only with four talismans, chosen by mystical means, Rowanda goes through a portal to Arolsen where her fate is intermingled with two desert dwellers. Together they join forces to brave the scorching desert days and frigid desert nights to rescue Rowanda's and her friend's mothers. Rowanda learns to use her magic to defend against nomads, desert serpents, sand dragons, and vicious felines.

The Palace City of Arolsen reveals the true identities of Rowanda's traveling companions and the reasons they accompanied her on her quest.

Find this book on Amazon, Kindle, Nook, and Barnes & Noble Now!

The Child Rowanda, Return to Arolsen
By
Carole Walker Carter

The Child Rowanda, Return to Arolsen,
Volume II, Alarm spreads through Neslora
as unexplained destruction occurs to the
bountiful planet. The Elder Sorceress
discovers the evil king, Nashua from
Arolsen is using charms Rowanda left for
her friend Boultori to use to turn their
barren desert into an oasis.

Now, Rowanda, with the help from her father, her grandmother, and
best friend, must right the wrong by retrieving Rowanda's talisman
and exchange them for charms that Boultori might use to overthrow
his evil brother's rule of Arolsen.

Two new talismans, chosen by magic, assist Rowanda as she learns to
control the most feared, yet fascinating creatures on Arolsen. These
creatures aide Rowanda on her quest for justice.

Magic abounds in this second book of the Child Rowanda series as
good battles evil to rescue a world from slavery and hardship and to
keep Neslora from the same predicament.

Find this book on Amazon, Kindle, Nook, and Barnes & Noble Now!

The Child Rowanda, Underworld
By
Carole Walker Carter

The Child Rowanda, Underworld, Volume III, Rowanda, attempts to rid the world of Neslora of the evil wizard, Nashua, Rowanda finds herself dragged into the Underworld with the evil sorcerer.

Navigating the terrifying darkness of this new world, Rowanda finds a mysterious and mystical guide who reveals that Rowanda can only exit the Underworld the same way she came in, with the evil sorcerer at her side. However, Nashua must be truly repentant of his depravities before he is allowed to leave, which means Rowanda cannot depart the Underworld if Nashua does not repent.

Trying to find Nashua in the darkness and convince him to repent, becomes a complicated and dangerous process. Making matters worse are the demons, intent on making both Nashua and Rowanda one of them, meaning living an eternity in the Underworld in agony.

Find this book on Amazon, Kindle, Nook, and Barnes & Noble Now!

Khaos, Lord of the Thunder Dragons
By
Carole Walker Carter

Khaos, Lord of the Thunder Dragons, is the prequel for *The Child Rowanda, Dragon Princess* book. Dragons have been depicted as monsters, devils, or even good-luck symbols throughout history. Dragons have been the focus of many stories throughout fictional and fantasy literature.

This is Khaos' story. Created by a mythological goddess, he is cast down with the lesser dragons to a world below. In this desert world, the dragons are thought of as either flesh-eating demons or good-luck omens. Differing labels are placed on these creatures, depending on the experiences of the nomads. Terms used include abductor, greedy hoarder, devourer, custodian of wisdom, guardian of the tree of life, chaos, as well as being symbols of good and evil.

You will find stories of brave young men, wanting to prove themselves and protect their villages, traveling to meet the monsters in battle, while others are rescued by the dragons and hold them in high reverence. Whatever men call Khaos, he remains, above all, the Lord of the Thunder Dragons.

The history of the dragon Khaos continues with many stories in these pages culminating in an encounter with Rowanda, the Dragon Princess. Here this story ends, but with more to be told by the many who will continue to encounter *Khaos, Lord of the Thunder Dragons*.

The Child Rowanda, Dragon Princess
By
Carole Walker Carter

The Child Rowanda, Dragon Princess, Volume IV. Leaving the Underworld through another portal, Rowanda finds she has not returned to her home-world of Neslora but finds herself on another parallel world with the devious Nashua. Here Rowanda is elevated to a princess.

Friends and members of her family are in this world, but they are not as they should be. They are doubles with a different personality and...no recollection of Rowanda.

Rowanda finds herself at odds with her look-alike parents, the king, and queen of Soleran.

Rowanda's magical talent of charming animals allows Rowanda to help the enslaved citizens of this world by joining the rebel army in opposition to the king and queen.

Wanting nothing more than to return to her own world, Rowanda seeks the aid of an ancient fire-breathing dragon.

Find this book on Amazon, Kindle, Nook, and Barnes & Noble Now!

Childhood Stories My Dad Told Me
By
Carole Walker Carter

Childhood Stories My Dad Told Me, is about growing up on a farm in Nebraska during the Great Depression. It was difficult, but for two young boys, life on the farm was also filled with fun and adventures.

This book is based on stories my dad told me about the amusing antics that he, his siblings, and friends found themselves in during these hard times.

The stories, filled with insights about rural schools, country social events, and harvest time, as well as the day-to-day chores of a working farm, are informative as well as enchanting.

Find this book on Amazon, Kindle, Nook, and Barnes & Noble Now!

www.ingramcontent.com/pod-product-compliance
Lightning Source LLC
Chambersburg PA
CBHW020434180626
46812CB00003B/1224